DEAD WOOD

Douglas Maas

Copyright © 2022 Douglas Maas

All rights reserved

The characters and events portrayed in this book are fictitious. Any similarity to real persons, living or dead, is coincidental and not intended by the author.

No part of this book may be reproduced, or stored in a retrieval system, or transmitted in any form or by any means, electronic, mechanical, photocopying, recording, or otherwise, without express written permission of the publisher.

CONTENTS

Title Page

Copyright

Dedication

NOTE TO READERS — 1

CHAPTER 1 — 3

CHAPTER 2 — 17

CHAPTER 3 — 37

CHAPTER 4 — 43

CHAPTER 5 — 52

CHAPTER 6 — 64

CHAPTER 7 — 77

CHAPTER 8 — 87

CHAPTER 9 — 108

CHAPTER 10 — 132

CHAPTER 11 — 143

CHAPTER 12 — 160

CHAPTER 13 — 176

CHAPTER 14	206
CHAPTER 15	228
CHAPTER 16	257
CHAPTER 17	292
EPILOGUE	312
About The Author	315

NOTE TO READERS

Market Easterby is the principal town of a modest English county. By stretching the imagination, it is possible to suppose the county might squeeze into a geographical area, somehow, between Norfolk, Cambridgeshire and Suffolk. It is an unassuming part of England which, if you didn't know the area, you would rarely ever think about. Travellers passing through give little thought to where they might be. Especially now, in the late 1970s, as the recently opened motorway speeds them to their destinations.

In the towns and villages, shops and pubs, industries and factories, farms and woodlands the lives of local people - villagers and townsfolk - are as they might be anywhere.

Work and play, joy and sadness, life and death ...

But that week in November would

change many lives.

CHAPTER 1

Bruce Morgan had always wanted to find a body. No, that overstates the case. There had been a time when the thought had, for some reason, excited his imagination. These days it occasionally crossed his mind. How would he feel at the time and afterwards? How would the experience affect him if he should actually find one? Presumably a murdered one. The body itself would not trouble him. He had seen and handled many dead bodies. No, it was about how he would deal with the fuss and questions. He doubted he would cope very well. No matter, such a thing was so unlikely.

The influence had of course been those TV crime dramas. Not the older shows, like 'Dixon of Dock Green', 'Z Cars' and the rest. They had been enjoyable but quite tame. The newer ones could become a bit macabre at times, even when viewed on his ageing black and white television. Usually, in a beautiful remote wood, someone would discover a pale hand sticking out from a pile of leaves. Or possibly a shoe or a boot but still containing the wearer's foot and leg. Maybe an arm would emerge from the water at the edge of a river at a crucial moment in front of a startled pair of furtive lovers. So often though, it seemed to involve woodland. The finder always seemed to scream at the top of their voice. That was just on television of course and seemed very silly. Bruce would never do that.

It was autumn now. The beginning of November. A keen wind whipped across the town under scudding dark grey clouds. Bruce shivered slightly but knew the walk would warm him up. He checked the collar of his warm green winter anorak was well fastened around his neck. This morning he wished he had selected a warmer jumper. He often misjudged the temperature. At least he had remembered to put on his grey woolly hat. He pulled it down over his ears.

His dog-walking duty took him, as usual most mornings, through a paved gap between two of the estate's semi-detached houses. The large area of empty land behind the houses had been planted with young trees years ago. These were intended as a barrier to hide the long artificial hill which in turn hid from sight the extensive factory which made concrete products.

When the trees were young, walking between

them was easy. Local kids had played their hide and seek games, making criss-crossing paths through the area and all over the hill. Those kids had grown up. The site became a rarely visited muddy waste land, with scrubby and broken trees, used mostly by dog walkers like Bruce. These days he found it tricky to trudge up the embankment and in any case the wind was bitter enough without him wanting to climb a hill.

Here, as always, he let Joe off the lead. Faithful Joe, a black Labrador, was content to follow the usual trail, never straying far. No further than the occasional new smell to sniff. Maybe a rabbit or a fox had passed through, if he was lucky.

This morning there was added interest for Joe. A lively young springer spaniel ran through the undergrowth towards him. They greeted one another as long lost friends.

"Tina … Tina …, here girl." The small man who was calling was wearing a heavy grey overcoat, scarf and a flat cap. From a distance he had spotted Joe and then Bruce. "Ah, it's you Bruce. Good morning. How are you doing now? Still improving? A bitter one this morning, isn't it?" Then adding, "Good boy, Joe."

"Morning, Dylan," said Bruce. The two men had a vague affinity, both having Welsh origins. "We don't often see you here these mornings. Must be a couple of weeks now. Yes, not bad thanks. Getting there."

"Good show. I'm usually about," Dylan pulled Tina's lead from his pocket. "Often earlier than this. Always jobs to do, you know. We don't always come this way anyway. Sometimes we have a change and jump in the car and go over to the Heath. Makes a change for you … doesn't it, Tina?"

"Will we see you at the *George* on Thursday?"

"Yes, I'll be there as usual. Hey, Tina, leave Joe alone. We're going now. Come here. Good dog." Dylan clipped Tina's lead to her collar to separate her from Joe.

"See you on Thursday then," said Bruce. They continued their walks in opposite directions.

Joe continued plodding along the trail. He stopped at the little gate which was barely attached with rusting hinges to the tired chestnut paling fence which stretched untidily across that end of the waste land. As always, Joe sat and waited for Bruce to reach the gate, unlatch and open it, so they could pass through.

Beyond the fence was mature woodland but it was not a beautiful wood in real countryside or as pictured on calendar pages. These few unhappy acres bordered the edge of the town which had encroached on the right, separated only by a grey close-boarded fence. To the left were the railway tracks which fed wagons into and out of the concrete factory.

Long ago, before houses and factories had crept up to it and destroyed most of it, the woodland had been left only to nature. For years now though, discarded junk had found its way there. Proud oaks had been damaged and graffiti carved into them. Many bore charred signs of attempts to set fire to them. Hardly anyone dared venture into a more remote corner where an ancient hollow sweet chestnut tree barely held on to life. Great care was needed around there to avoid the discarded detritus left lying around by folk who, increasingly these days, felt that taking drugs was the way. Or whatever else it was they got up to in that woodland seclusion.

Whatever was going on there was making local folk uneasy.

Not far away hangs a makeshift swing seat suspended on frayed ropes from a high branch. A child's pink bicycle, rusted and bent, lies abandoned in a bramble patch which has not yet quite consumed it. The fence on the left, separating the railway sidings, is barely visible under a mass of impenetrable undergrowth. Bruce often thought that someone should tidy up the place so the few birds, butterflies and the occasional fox and other mammals could enjoy a nicer home.

Joe was constantly hunting for a new place to sniff. He followed Bruce's steady saunter along the flattened earth track. It was the mid-morning quiet time while children were at school. The temporary shelter from the wind was welcome, though brown leaves fluttered constantly to the ground. A growling diesel shunting engine disturbed the peace, towing its clanking squeaking wagons.

Some distance before the end of the track, the trees thinned out. A pile of dead branches, old and broken wooden boxes and some bits of broken furniture had been assembled in the small clearing. Day by day, Bruce had watched the pile grow bigger. Bonfire night was tomorrow, Wednesday. He hoped the fire would not get out of hand.

From the clearing, on the right and almost invisible unless you know it is there, a little path wanders through dense undergrowth. Some local people have always known it as a shortcut to and from the town. There used to be a proper gate until the council replaced the fence separating the wood from the town. For some reason the gate was omitted. Vandals quickly created the narrow gap so the shortcut was retained.

Bruce and Joe continued onwards to where there are some rusty black iron railings. An iron gate gives access to Beech Street.

The two facing rows of terraced houses were built around the turn of the century for workers at the new factories and warehouses. Victorian industry and enterprise had been in full swing. Beech Street is one of a dozen, all with tree names, closely packed into this corner of town. Forest Road leads into the town centre.

Bruce smiled to himself, remembering when he and Jennifer had married just after the War and had rented one of those houses in Ash Street for a few years. It hadn't been easy in such a tiny house to bring up their two babies.

To the left, a high concrete and graffiti covered wall broods over the end of Beech Street. It encloses those ever-present railway sidings. Standing back a bit, all one can see over the wall is the top of a solitary railway signal, marking the junction of the factory sidings with the main line. Trains pass occasionally and the signal raises its red arm in anticipation, bouncing back to the horizontal when the train has passed on its way to Millwood Station.

Unseen from here, beyond the railway, are the vast green acres and distant grey buildings of the RAF base which had been Bruce's all-consuming life many years ago. He had happy memories of his life at the base for all those years. It was where he had met Jennifer.

These days there is a lot of pilot training at

RAF Millwood, often involving repeated fly-overs by the trainees doing their take-off and landing routines. Hereabouts the distant background noise is accepted but occasionally a pilot would break the unwritten rule and fly over the town making people duck and clasp hands over their ears.

Closing the gate, Bruce glanced across the road at the pair of sad terraced houses at the end, the ones with grimy windows and fading yellowing curtains. Next to them, a long high brick wall fills the gap before the next houses. Within the wall are large brown double gates with peeling paint. A faded yellow sign, 'Tallows Metal Dealers', indicates this is the entrance to a scrap yard. It amused Bruce as it reminded him of 'Steptoe and Son' on television. Folk generally considered the place to be rather unsavoury and kept away. The Tallows themselves were seldom seen.

Clipping Joe's lead to his collar once more, they turned to face the wind funnelling down Beech Street. Their daily walk usually followed the same route. In their car owning days, they would sometimes enjoy a run into the country. Joe used to like that and so did Bruce and Jennifer. But now, from Beech Street they turned right into Forest Road, passing the telephone box and to the corner shop to pick up a newspaper and maybe some tobacco. Then a short walk through the Square, past the *George and Dragon* and

Tesco's and a few other shops. About ten minutes later they arrived home at 33 Lyndon Avenue where Bruce and Jennifer had lived for more than 25 years.

Bruce was glad he was able to enjoy his walks with Joe. With winter approaching he also enjoyed returning home to settle down for an hour or so with his paper, a mug of his favourite coffee and one of his occasional pipefuls of St. Bruno flake. Joe would rest his head on Bruce's knee for a while before settling down on the rug for a snooze.

For just a brief moment, Bruce was puzzled. Why had he noted such a particular minor detail today? Thinking back, he recalled there had been broken glass on the pavement next to the telephone box near the corner shop. One of the small glass panes had been smashed.

That other thought only rarely occurred to him these days. The one about wondering what it would be like to find a dead body. It had not done so this morning.

Jennifer liked to have the house to herself for a while each morning. Her second cup of tea of the day, enjoyed in peace, with the tick of the hall clock for company. She usually got on with the morning chores, making the bed, washing the breakfast things. If the weather was good she might delay all that and potter about in the modest garden to tidy a flower bed and put out some scraps for the birds. Perhaps Bruce would wash up the breakfast things when he got home, while she finished in the garden. Sometimes he did.

During her morning quiet time, Jennifer would occasionally find herself reflecting on her life with Bruce. It had begun dramatically enough, during the War. At the age of 22 she had somehow been swept up from her typist's desk at the office of a small firm making scientific instruments. It had all happened so quickly. As the War progressed, women were called up, either to factory work or the armed forces. She was thankful she had ended up in the Women's Auxiliary Air Force rather than a factory. She had been posted to RAF Millwood, a base about 80 miles from where she lived in the Midlands with her parents.

From RAF Millwood, amongst other missions, reconnaissance flights took off and landed at frequent intervals. The small aeroplanes, Spitfires and others, sometimes with only the pilot and sometimes with an observer, were sent on those hazardous missions over enemy territory to photograph potential bombing targets. Jennifer worked in the laboratory where the secret photographs were processed.

The cameras used were specialised affairs, constantly being modified and improved. They were loaded with film and bolted into the belly, sides and sometimes the rear of the aircraft. When the aircraft returned, technicians would retrieve the cameras, rushing them to the laboratory.

One of the technicians always smiled at Jennifer in a certain way. This had led, bit by bit, to fingers touching hands during the handover. Jennifer came to realise that Sergeant Bruce Morgan was an attractive proposition. With a silent chuckle to herself she remembered that first occasion when she had allowed him to join her in the darkroom for the process of removing the film from a camera into the developing tank. The precious film had not been the only precious thing to be fondled that day.

Of course, her colleagues soon guessed that Bruce was not merely interested in how the film was developed in the darkroom. Everyone was making liaisons in those tense days and finding their own ways of doing it. It was the thing to do. There was a war on.

Jennifer again caught herself smiling at her thoughts and just then heard Bruce and Joe arriving home. It was a regular routine. She made the coffee. "A good walk?" she asked.

"Um, yes. A bit chilly."

The daily walk with Joe had become so routine over the years, so automatic, that Bruce realised he could seldom remember what had happened between leaving home and returning back there. He decided he must be getting old.

"I got the paper." Bruce held it up. Jennifer told him to enjoy his coffee while she finished off in the garden. Even on such a windy day she had managed to gather up some fallen leaves.

Jennifer was wakeful that night, for no good reason. Her thoughts strayed back to those of the morning, thinking of her early days with Bruce and of how they had met. After leaving school at sixteen, Bruce had worked in a grocery shop in a small town in the North of England. Eventually - it was the mid-1930s - he had decided he wanted to be rid of the tedium and applied to join the Royal Air Force which seemed to be heavily recruiting. There was talk of trouble brewing on the Continent.

Bruce had told Jennifer of his ambition to fly and about being disappointed at not making the grade to become a pilot. However he had agreed to join up in a ground-based role. Being in the RAF was the thing. This is how he had come to be recruited into the technical department at RAF Millwood. He would be involved with aerial reconnaissance and photography. Bruce had proved to be a valuable member of the team and by the time War was declared in 1939, he had become Sergeant Morgan.

Bruce and Jennifer had waited to marry until shortly after the War had ended. They had rented a small house in the nearby town of Millwood. Jennifer's WAAF service had come to an end. Bruce had stayed on until 1948, only then deciding it would now be best to discover civilian life. The local paper was advertising vacancies for ambulance crews for the newly formed ambulance service. His rudimentary first-aid training at the air base had interested him and given him an RAF first-aid certificate. He would still be in uniform and working shifts. The ambulance service seemed keen to recruit ex-services personnel. He got the job and never looked back, retiring eventually just two years ago.

Their two children, Linda and Steven, had arrived during the four years they had lived at the tiny place in Ash Street. Eventually they bought the much nicer 1930's house in which they still lived. It was modest and adequate for their growing family. Lyndon Avenue was peaceful which was helpful when Bruce had been on night shifts. The children had married and now had homes of their own.

Jennifer, lying in bed close to Bruce, felt warm and cosy as these thoughts filtered through her mind, drifting her off to sleep. Like most folk in

Millwood, the family had, over the years, grown accustomed to ignoring the noise of those jet trainer flights. Now, even the pair of low-flying jets doing their night exercise circuits, didn't wake her.

CHAPTER 2

"Bloody drugs." Detective Inspector John Merton sounded seriously frustrated as he almost shouted the words. He was a stocky, medium-height, balding man in a grey suit in his early fifties. Two fingers of his right hand were pulling at his tight shirt collar as he read through the new day's routine crime reports.

"Sir?" Detective Sergeant Dave Harris looked up from the desk opposite. Harris was an experienced younger detective, tall and slim, in a light grey suit. With a telephone receiver to his ear, he had made an early start on a series of calls to pawnbrokers and second-hand shops in West Division This was a long-shot bid to track down some jewellery and silver, nicked in a series of recent burglaries. Finding the stolen gear might offer a clue to which of the local petty villains had been at work.

Such a ring-round was routine stuff which would usually be handled by DC Harlow. But Detective Constable Richard Harlow had been given a couple of days off to nurse a seriously bruised elbow. He'd incurred that in a spectacular rugby-tackle bringing a local tearaway to the ground. At least he had made a successful arrest which, with luck, should clear up a dozen or more outstanding car crime cases. DI Merton was pleased. Keeping the statistics looking good was, after all, the name of the game.

"Well, they complicate things, don't they? Bloody drugs," Merton repeated, calming down a bit but stating the obvious really. "It used to be just straightforward thieving. We used to understand one another, them and us. Petty stuff. Now it's all different because of all these bleary-eyed, low-life, hippy types taking trips on acid or whatever they do. They have to thieve to get the money to buy the stuff."

He was only stating what all detectives knew but for some reason he needed to get his frustration off his chest that Tuesday morning.

As if there wasn't enough on without being a man down and having been summoned to something called a 'review meeting' at Constabulary HQ this afternoon "at 1430 sharp", he had been told. Merton wanted to get stuck into the ongoing jobs, plus today's new crop, without having to kick his heels at a meeting all afternoon, 20 miles away. But he had a plan.

DI Merton extracted six of the reports and chucked the rest in a file tray which already contained quite a number. They would have to wait. The Division really did need one or two more detectives. Could this review meeting be about that? He could live in hope.

He called sharply across the CID office, "Taylor!"

"Sir?" A slim young woman wearing a white blouse and a grey skirt paused and turned. She was standing at the large pin board on the wall. The board was used to plot the progress of more complex cases such as murders, using maps and photographs. So far in her career Taylor had never been directly involved in such a case. Today, she was no closer as there was nothing on the board. She had been filling in time by tidying away some remaining drawing pins, putting them in a glass dish on a nearby table.

WPC Carol Taylor had been on the force only three and a half years when she had shown an interest in the CID. She had proved capable of pursuing the type of criminal every uniformed officer encountered on the beat. She remembered the faces of bicycle thieves and even those who stole milk bottles from doorsteps.

When the possibility of joining the CID has arisen she knew this would be a big step, not just for her as a young constable but also for the Force. There had long been female constables who always proved useful in situations involving women and children. But in this Force female detectives were almost unheard of.

Having arrived at West Division CID less than two weeks ago she was just beginning to get used to the characters in the office and how things worked. She hoped she was dressing appropriately. She was having doubts about the white and grey which seemed to hark back to uniform days. Maybe she would do it differently tomorrow. Men had it easy. She went over to DI Merton's desk. "Sir," she said again and waited.

"Any luck?" DI Merton addressed his question to Sergeant Harris.

"There might be one possible at a second-hand shop over in Millwood. It's called, er ... 'Second Chance'. That's original, I don't think," said Harris.

"Right. You're in charge later. I'm at HQ for 1400 and won't be back today. Take Taylor with you and show her the ropes at your second-hand shop. While you're in that neck of the woods you can follow up on these." He handed Harris the six messages. "Reports of drug use increasing. Locals upset. You know the kind of thing. Call at the local Nick and see if their uniform can throw any light."

"Right Sir." Harris gave Taylor the messages to look over while he went back to finishing off the phone calls. Sergeant Harris was thorough.

The arrival of Taylor in the office had caused some uncertainty, not least about what to call her. Whereas WPC was commonly used for uniformed female officers, there was no precedent for a female detective constable to be called WDC. It was a new phenomenon. So, for now, Detective Constable Carol Taylor was just called Taylor.

Taylor sat at the table near the pin board. She studied the messages, all from people living in an area of Millwood around Forest Road. There were two in Beech Street. This was unfamiliar territory to her. A far cry from urban Central Division. These good folk were reporting suspicious activity in some woods next to Beech Street. They alleged that youngsters were using drugs. Residents were getting uneasy and wanted it stopped.

Merton got into his usual muddle, trying to return some files to a filing cabinet. This time it was probably because he was in a hurry. He told Taylor to do the job. He looked up at the office clock which said 1150 and said to Harris, "I'd better be off. Don't dwell too long on that Millwood thing. Anyway, keep your radio on in case anything kicks off. See you tomorrow."

"Right-oh, Sir," said Sergeant Harris.

"Sir," said Taylor.

DI Merton, carrying the battered briefcase he brought out for meetings, was still pulling on his overcoat as he went through the door.

Soon afterwards, in the car park at Divisional Headquarters, DS Harris and DC Taylor were in one of the two pool cars allocated to the CID office. These cars were swapped around occasionally between divisions and departments. It wouldn't do for the criminal fraternity to become too familiar with which cars CID were driving. Sergeant Harris had switched on his pocket Pye two-way radio. He told Divisional Control, "Sergeant Harris and DC Taylor on inquiries at Millwood." "Roger," crackled the reply.

"Enjoying it?" asked Harris. "CID, I mean."

"Yes, Sarge. Thank you. Well, once I get some proper work to do."

Harris steered the car onto the main road to the small town of Millwood, six miles away. "Well, today's routine but it's a proper job. Checking out the Second Chance shop might get interesting if they've actually got any of that gear. Might lead to an arrest or two."

"Yes, Sarge." Taylor was still weighing up her relationship with these detectives. They appeared to operate in unexpected ways she wasn't at all familiar with.

"We don't need to be formal when we're out and about like this. I'm Dave."

"Okay Sar … Dave," said Taylor. "Carol," she added, catching his eye. She thought Dave Harris was nice but she had also quickly worked out he was a lot older and appeared to be engaged. In any case, she didn't want to get involved just yet. Or did she? She wasn't quite sure.

The second-hand shop fascia board over the shop window was in a faded yellow colour with the words 'Second Chance' in large black letters. The young man in the shop, Russell, appeared quite nervous. He seemed uncertain of his ground when confronted with the fact he had acquired some hot property which was about to be removed from his premises by the police. The few pieces of silver he had were nowhere near all of the gear they were hoping to find. He had no knowledge of any more and promised he would learn quickly from his mistake. Harris had let Taylor do much of the interview. He was impressed. She knew her stuff and was clearly pleased to be getting into this kind of policing at the sharp end. In the coming days she wanted to be part of the round-up and prosecution of the thieves.

Harris locked the recovered valuables securely into the boot of the pool car. "We'd better get moving. It gets dark early these days. We might need a look at these woods they're talking about."

He drove to the small police station just off the Square. Inside, he asked if they had received complaints about drug taking around Beech Street. "I think so," the constable at the inquiry desk said. "Hang on, I'll ask PC Stevens. He's on the beat down there today." A radio call later and they had arranged to meet PC Stevens in Beech Street.

Harris knew where to find Forest Road. It left the town square by the side of the small Tesco's branch. There were several streets named after trees, he recalled.

Having found Beech Street, Harris parked the car. PC Stevens was there. "Afternoon Sergeant." He nodded to Taylor in a way which acknowledged he had never seen a plain clothes woman constable before.

"All quiet?" asked Harris.

"Yep, not a lot doing around here on week days, unless you count the factories turning out from about 1600, especially on Fridays. Then there's always inquiries going on about the usual petty stuff."

"Livens up at night then, does it?"

"Well, a bit. We mostly use the panda cars then. Usually a few disturbances, drunks later on. The usual, really," concluded PC Stevens.

"What about complaints about drug taking around here? Is there a problem?"

"Ah yes," remembered Stevens. "I've been stopped in the street a few times lately. I took a walk through the wood the other day. There's a place where there must have been something going on. A bit messy. Had to be careful. Nobody about though."

No, thought Harris, you wouldn't see anybody about while you're driving around in a nice warm panda car. "Let's try having a word with one or two of these," he said, bringing out the messages. He had already glanced at the street plan and knew roughly where the wood was. "Number 42. That should be on the left. It presumably backs onto the wood. They might even have a view of what's going on."

A woman wearing a multicoloured apron and a green head scarf had suddenly appeared. She stepped up onto some short stepladders on the pavement, appearing to be cleaning the windows of number 42.

"Good afternoon," said Harris, carefully avoiding startling her, "Mrs Robertson?"

Stepping down to the pavement, she turned to Stevens, put her hands on her hips and scowled. "Did you ever do anything about those hippies in the wood? It's still going on you know. You never know what they might be up to."

Taylor took the initiative, "Hello, Mrs Robertson. We're detectives. We're here about some reports made to headquarters. I think you made one of those calls. We're here to look into it. What have you seen?"

"It would be really helpful if you could tell us exactly," added Harris.

Mrs. Robertson softened. Detectives, she thought, feeling the buzz of being important. Her neighbours would take note. She turned her back on PC Stevens and said, "I would never go into that wood. It's creepy. You can see it best from upstairs. Back bedroom window."

"Sorry to impose but would you mind showing us, please?" asked Taylor.

PC Stevens removed his helmet, tucking it under his arm. Mrs. Robertson led the way down a narrow entry, through the back gate into a small yard and into the kitchen. This led to a tiny back room with a table, two armchairs and a TV set. They all went up the dark narrow stairs. The landing led to a door into an untidy room at the back of the house.

"Don't mind my Rosie's stuff. She'll be home from school in a bit."

They barely fitted into this box room. Mrs. Robertson pointed out of the window. "It's over there." Harris and Taylor squashed together by the window and took in the scene. The back yard ended in a brick wall which extended to right and left, unbroken, along the backs of all the houses in the street. Beyond the wall was the wood. It all looked much the same - lots of trees, large bushes and undergrowth. A bit untidy and maybe 'creepy' as Mrs. Robertson had said. Peering around to the right, in the distance, they could just make out some railway wagons on a track a little way beyond an overgrown fence. Gradually they picked out some detail. In the near distance there was clearly the makings of quite a large a bonfire, being built within a small clearing.

"Perhaps that needs keeping an eye on tomorrow night, Stevens, don't you think?"

"Yes Sarge," said PC Stevens, a bit hesitant as he was not used to receiving instructions from plain clothes sergeants.

"It's over there." Mrs Robertson pointed more to the left. It was just possible to pick out what she meant, through the trees, at least 200 yards away. There seemed to be a rough circle of big fallen branches around a very large tree, not easy to pick out in the gathering gloom. At ground level you would need to be very close to be able to see it all.

"You can see them at night with their torches and lighters and whatever," said Mrs. Robertson. "I wouldn't go near it myself. You don't know what they get up to."

Sergeant Harris had got the picture and didn't need to see any more. He told Mrs. Robertson he would keep in touch with PC Stevens who would keep her and the other complainants informed of any action to be taken.

After thanking Mrs. Robertson, they walked a short distance along the street. Stevens made a note of the details of the other five complainants so he could tell them that CID was on the case. He left them and continued walking his beat, which would now take him steadily towards the Nick and his 45 minute break. The remainder of his duty until 2200 hours would be in a panda car. "What on earth can anybody do about what goes on in that wood at night?" he was thinking. Perhaps he should freshen up his knowledge of the law about drugs. Out here in the sticks it was a new thing.

Sergeant Harris had come to a similar conclusion. What exactly could be done? How much of a problem is it, really? He and Taylor walked to the end of Beech Street, stopping by the iron gate. Street lights had come on. It would be dark in half an hour. "To be honest, I don't think we'll see much more if we go in there now," he said. "We've got the lay of the land. I'll run it all past the DI when I get the chance."

Taylor had been looking around. "If anyone actually sees what goes on it's likely to be them." She was pointing across the road to the brown gates. Her voice was almost drowned out by the diesel shunting engine and a train of clanking wagons.

"Yes, good thinking Carol. They must be around quite a bit." They crossed the street. Harris used his fist to bang on the brown gates of the scrap yard, noting the yellow sign, 'Tallows Metal Dealers'. Taylor peered into the window of the adjacent house with the grimy windows and yellowing curtains. She rapped the knocker on the front door. A faint light appeared behind the window and the door opened a few inches. Harris had joined her and they showed their warrant cards.

The door opened a few inches more and a thin, rather grimy young man appeared in the dim light. "Sorry to disturb you, Sir," said Harris, "We're making inquiries about reports of activity in the wood over the road. Have you seen anything unusual going on?"

"I'll fetch me Dad." The young man was gone. A bent old man, equally grimy, appeared. Harris repeated the question.

"There's always folk in and out the wood," said Mr. Tallow. "Don't bother us. Don't know anything else."

Instinctively Harris knew that this line would draw a blank. "Thanks for your help." Harris wanted to be gone. He would be away on his two days' leave tomorrow and the next day. That was on his mind.

On the drive back in the dark, Harris said, "I don't know what we're supposed to do with all this, Carol. Merton's quite right - drugs, just a bloody nuisance to us. Why they do it, goodness only knows. I'll run it past him next time I see him. But I've got a couple of days' leave now. House hunting, would you believe?"

Taylor smiled. That answered one question anyway. After parking the car at DHQ, they booked the property recovered from Second Chance into the property room. Harris told Taylor she might as well get off home and he would finish in the office. He added that he expected DC

Harlow should be back tomorrow, if his elbow was okay. "You'll be able to get your teeth into rounding up some jewellery thieves. See if you can find out where the rest of the stuff is. You're in the big time now, eh?" he chuckled.

The business of the drugs in the wood could wait until he was back after his leave. Dave Harris's mind was on some rare quality time, house hunting with his fiancé, Susan.

He would be back in the office on Friday morning.

◆ ◆ ◆

DI Merton, having struggled into his overcoat, had left the office, leaving Harris and Taylor to their afternoon inquiries in Millwood. He briskly descended the stairs, waved at the desk sergeant who tried to catch his attention but missed his opportunity, left the building and strode across to his car.

The black Rover P6 purred at a steady 50mph along the main road towards the County town, Market Easterby. He hadn't remembered to switch his own pocket radio on.

John Merton had once been married. That hadn't gone well. Nobody needed to know the sordid details, he had decided, so nobody got told them. For the past 15 years or so he had been on his own. Looking after himself was not easy but that was nobody's business. After all, work kept him busy. Inevitably people noticed that his catering seemed to mostly involve pubs, fish and chip shops, burger bars and transport cafes. No wonder his shirt collars always seemed to be a bit tight.

Today, his immediate target was the *White Horse*, a red brick roadhouse at the big roundabout where the slip road to the new M19 motorway connected on the outskirts of Market Easterby. It was an anonymous sort of place with mostly passing trade in the daytime. The cooking was good enough. Very rarely would anyone there recognise DI Merton but on the other hand, if he chose his table carefully, he could keep an eye open for known faces, as they passed through. The strategy had worked well for him a few times in the past. Being a detective was John Merton's life. He was always on duty.

He checked his watch as his cottage pie and chips arrived at his table. It was just after 1245. There were no interruptions today. He decided one pint was enough, given he had got the darned meeting with the Super. He would be at Headquarters by 1400 so he could look in on his old mate, Frank Leeman, before going into the meeting.

He and Frank had been detectives together.

There was that fateful day when Frank had been shot in the thigh by a fleeing armed robber. He had recovered reasonably well, though his leg was never going to be good enough for active policing again. Eventually he had accepted promotion to the lighter duty role of Control Room Inspector.

Earlier, John had made a call and knew that Frank would come on duty for the 1400 to 2200 shift. He left the *White Horse,* turned out of the car park and headed the Rover for Headquarters.

London Road in Market Easterby was once the wealthy neighbourhood in town where, in times past, business and professional people used to own enormous houses in large grounds. The growing County Constabulary had purchased one of the largest ones as its headquarters building. It sat behind elegant railings and mature trees and bushes which concealed the building from the road. Massive iron gates made for an ostentatious entrance.

DI Merton turned the Rover through the gates, past the large 'Constabulary Headquarters' signs and up the curving drive to a small car park adjacent to the buildings. Over the years, many brick-built extensions had been added, turning what was once an elegant stone-built residence into an ugly jumble.

He walked around a corner to a long two-storey brick building which sported an array of radio aerials on top. Inside, he climbed the stairs. There was the continuous clatter of teleprinters in a room to the left of the landing. He turned to a door on the right and pressed an intercom button. "Control Room," said the loudspeaker. "DI Merton to see Inspector Leeman." There was a loud click. He pushed the door open just as Frank was coming to greet him. "It's been a while." "How're you doing?" "Good to see you," they were saying.

"Just thought I'd call in, as I'm here for a meeting. Checking up on you." They laughed. The chatting went on for a while in the low tones which were necessary in that room.

Merton glanced up at the large clear calendar clock which said "TUES" on the top line, "4 NOV" on the next line and "14:07" below that.

Frank had once explained to him the mysteries of how it all worked. The dominant feature was the long curved desk with six positions facing the wall with the clock. Below the clock was an electronic display showing the state of all the available mobile units. To the left was a large-scale map of the County. To the right, recently added, was a tall white board depicting the new M19 motorway and its junctions, as it passed through the County.

Each of the six desks was a mini switchboard

with rows of small lamps indicating a call - flashing if it needed answering or steady for a call in progress. The several '999' lines had red lamps. The operators at the two middle desks would normally operate the Force radio channels. They would often listen in to 999 calls and have police cars on the way as soon as a location had been given.

Below each desk were two drawers. The top one contained a series of files, each covering actions to be followed in various serious or complex situations, such as a plane or train crash. Merton had wondered if there was a file marked 'Murder'. There couldn't be a standard set of actions for that, he had mused. The lower drawers each held a sophisticated voice recorder which recorded everything that was said at that desk together with the date and time.

Today there were five operators. Three were police constables in uniform shirt sleeve order. The other two were civilian control assistants. As messages came in, they wrote the details on standard A4 message forms, together with the actions they had taken.

Overlooking the long room, at the back, was an almost identical desk but raised on a dais. This is where the Control Room Inspector sat, supervising everything. He could listen in to any call going on.

In the corner was the Sergeant's desk. He continuously checked the messages to be sure all necessary actions had been taken. There were hundreds every day. Some reported serious crime and emergency situations. Most were routine.

"I'd better be gone," Merton glanced again at the clock. "Good to see you. Let's meet up for a drink sometime." "Good idea, mate," said Frank.

DI Merton crossed the yard to the main building, the original old house with its still grand interiors. He went through a door and into the meeting, still not sure what a 'review meeting' would be all about.

CHAPTER 3

Wednesday was the fifth of November. Since last week the high winds and overcast skies had given way to frosty mornings and hazy sunshine. Bruce and Joe returned from their morning walk just before eleven o'clock. Joe sat on the rug in front of Bruce's special armchair. Bruce stood in the hall with Joe's lead in his hand.

"I've made your coffee," Jennifer said, bringing it through to the sitting room. Bruce remained standing in the hall.

"What's the matter dear?"

"Um." Bruce looked as though he was trying to remember something. Jennifer had noticed more and more, especially this year, that Bruce seemed to be quite aimless. Often preoccupied and forgetful.

"The paper," Bruce said. "I remembered the

bank but forgot to pick up the paper. How stupid am I?" He still had his overcoat on. "I'll go back for it now. Won't be long."

Jennifer considered whether to pour the coffee away and make another when Bruce got back. Or should she re-heat the first one in a saucepan? She began, once again, to try to think of ways she could get her husband to be more interested in things. His job had been his life. Over the years he had been promoted, retiring with the rank of Station Officer. He had got involved in everything, even after his normal shifts. He did as much overtime as he could, when it came his way. He had volunteered to help train people in first aid, judge competitions for youth groups and so on. He had never really had time for other hobbies, beyond some essential DIY at home. He wasn't very good at that.

She knew he hated being retired. They didn't do much together other than the routine at home. It didn't help not having a car now. The trusty Hillman Minx had served them reliably for many years and had lasted just long enough to get Bruce to and from work. Then he said it could never pass another MOT test without spending a small fortune on it. They had agreed a car was not really essential, living as they did within 10 minutes' walk of the town centre. Bruce had said his pensions were not enough to buy another car and run it, especially with still having the mortgage for two or three more years. Maybe then.

Joe didn't get up from the rug to greet Bruce when he returned with the paper, as though admonishing him for not taking him along. Bruce lit his pipe and settled into his chair with the freshly made coffee Jennifer had brought him. He read his paper from cover to cover.

***

It was barely dark when the fireworks began. Joe's ears pricked up at the first sounds of rockets, bangers and jump-jacks. Nowadays he was wise enough to know it wasn't worth bothering about.

Jennifer said, "It'll be dark in a few minutes. Shall we go upstairs and watch?"

In recent years they had enjoyed watching the spectacle spread around the back gardens of the nearby streets. Roman candles, Catherine wheels and rockets lit up the sky. They had once done all that themselves, with the children, inviting neighbours around and enjoying a drink and some hot dogs. They even had a small bonfire in the garden, burning a Guy Fawkes on top, which Linda and Steven had made. Happy times.

"Alright." Bruce was a little bemused they could still enjoy it. They sat on the bed in the back bedroom with the light switched off and watched through the window as the night sky was lit up as far as they could see.

"How about a glass of wine?" said Jennifer, out of the blue.

"Have we got any?" Bruce said, knowing it wasn't usual these days.

"I brought one home with me from work." Jennifer had worked part-time as a checkout operator at Tesco's since the store opened a few years ago,. It helped with the grocery shopping, especially with her staff discount.

She had thought the wine would cheer him up a bit. In any case, she wanted him in a good mood. Returning with the bottle and two glasses, she gave Bruce the bottle. "I've uncorked it. You pour it," she said, "It's your favourite, Bordeaux."

"Wasn't that expensive?"

"Doesn't matter. It's my treat."

Jennifer put the glasses on the dressing table and Bruce carefully poured. They sipped, still watching fireworks lighting up the sky. They even had another half glass each, agreeing to keep the remainder of the bottle to have with Sunday dinner.

"I've been thinking, Bruce," said Jennifer. "Do you think we should have a proper holiday next year? Nothing expensive. A week at the seaside would be really nice."

When the children were young they had seaside holidays, sometimes twice a year. There were many fond memories. As Linda and Steven grew into independent teenagers, eventually leaving home, the habit had gradually stopped. It wasn't Jennifer. Bruce seemed to lose interest in the idea. He found excuses.

"Mmm, yes it would be a good idea. It will be easier though, when the mortgage is paid off. We'll think about it."

Three years ago and with retirement and a reduced income looming, Bruce had said it would be best to extend the mortgage on the house by five years. "Spread the cost," he had said. Jennifer had questioned it and didn't really like the idea. But she tended to leave the financial decisions to Bruce. She didn't understand all that very well.

Now, Jennifer thought Bruce's reply gave a glimmer of hope and she would remember to suggest it again after Christmas.

◆ ◆ ◆

The bonfire in the woodland clearing burned well, fireworks lit up the sky and children from the nearby streets enjoyed themselves. PC Stevens did drive his panda car along Beech Street, got out, stood by the railings and watched for a while until the fire had burned down and the Guy was no more. All was well.

CHAPTER 4

Detective Constable Harlow decided his elbow needed an extra day to heal sufficiently, before returning to duty. Therefore it was Thursday before he and Taylor were able to get together to assemble what evidence they had and go after the jewellery and silver thieves. Much of the day was spent doing just that. Without more of the stolen gear, they mainly followed blind alleys. All the usual local suspects appeared to have plausible alibis. For now at least.

◆ ◆ ◆

Once more, Jennifer was worrying about Bruce's forgetfulness. That morning, he'd forgotten to pick up the newspaper again and seemed more morose than ever.

"Cheer up," she said, "it's Thursday. You'll enjoy your night out."

Jennifer's words made Bruce's mind hark back to those Thursday nights which began as long ago as any of the friends could remember. Goodness - almost 30 years. Nearly as far back as their RAF days. A few of the lads had left the Service at a similar time and six had remained living either in Millwood or nearby. The friends stayed in touch. Some had married more or less immediately, like Bruce, others later. Jim never did get married and always proclaimed himself as the happy bachelor.

Inevitably, they met socially. For a while it had been quite ad hoc, on different days and at different pubs or for a walk in the Summer or at somebody's house. After a year or two, they agreed it made sense to stick to the same day and place. The obvious place had become the *George and Dragon* and Thursday was the day which suited them all.

The group evolved. The original link, their RAF service, was ever present and the main topic of conversation in the earlier days. As the years passed, other regulars in the bar showed an interest, a few gradually became friends and were absorbed into the group. Some years ago, somebody had the idea of forming a darts team. One thing led to another and they found themselves in the County League. On the second Thursday of the month they played another team, either home or away. It was serious business. They began to call themselves, informally, the Thursday Club.

It had always been a male group, for no particular reason. It was just how it was, until Raymond had brought his wife Janet along. Just to say hello, she had said. The evening had gone well and somehow, quite naturally, Janet became a regular attender. She wasn't bad at darts either.

A younger woman often seemed to be in the bar of the *George and Dragon* on those Thursdays, seemingly on her own. One evening she had approached the group and told them her name was Sally. She had said she couldn't help noticing the dart-playing group and told them she was a pretty good shot with an arrow and wondered if they would let her have a go. "Double-top Sally, they used to call me," she had laughed. Sally clearly possessed certain attractions for a group of middle-aged men who were all 10 or 15 years older than her. They were too polite to ask but most of them guessed correctly that Sally was in her mid-thirties then. Her bold approach had stunned them into silence until Jim had spoken up, "Let me get you a drink." Of course, one thing led to another. Sally had proved to be an invaluable member of the darts team and seemed to slip naturally into the group. The men were only too pleased to welcome her. It was all quite innocent. She had told them she had been married but was no longer and she was enjoying her life as much as possible. She was fun and they enjoyed her lively company. And she was a really good darts player.

That was all a long time ago. The Thursday Club seemed to go on and on. Inevitably, in that time, some of the friends had died or otherwise stepped down. Occasionally another would join. Bruce was just one of the three remaining ex-RAF friends who had started it all.

Bruce had been lost in these thoughts. "My night out?" he said. "Oh yes, I see. Thursday. Yes, it is, isn't it?"

"It's nearly half past six." Jennifer reminded him. "Do you really want to go tonight? It's getting really cold outside now and it'll be frosty when you come home. You'll have to take care in case the pavement's slippery. Make sure you've got your scarf and woolly hat. Have you got your wallet?"

"Yes, got to go." Bruce was a bit irritated at the fussing but Jennifer knew he would forget something if she didn't. He was glad she had reminded him of the time. Jennifer was looking forward to settling down with a library book. Pouring a glass of wine had crossed her mind but no, she wouldn't. They had agreed to keep the remainder to have with Sunday dinner.

They kissed and Bruce left the house for the

ten minute walk into town. The others usually started to arrive at the *George and Dragon* from about quarter to seven. Most walked but a few came by car from the far side of town or from an outlying village. Usually there were one or two who couldn't make it for some reason so the usual group varied around eight or nine.

Fred was already there, at the bar. He was usually early, his plan being that if he bought an early round before everyone got there it would be a cheaper one.

"Hello Fred," said Bruce, "How are you? My usual pint please. Thanks."

Raymond and Janet came through the other door, from the car park. "A bit chilly. Oh, thanks Fred. A pint and a port and lemon please."

Jim arrived next and was happy the take over from Fred, buying the drinks for himself and Rob and Dylan who arrived just after him.

"Are you trying to bankrupt me, Lucy?" Jim sounded truly offended as he addressed the barmaid with a wink. "Forty pea! You've put the price of a pint up again!" It was the usual good-natured banter. Lucy knew he wasn't serious. She glanced along the bar at Geoffrey, the landlord. He stood there with a knowing smile.

The early arrivals stood around at the bar chatting about the weather and how they were doing. They gradually moved to sit at their usual large table alongside the dart board.

Just before 7.30, Sally walked through the room towards them. Even all these years later she drew admiring glances, as she slipped off her warm, wool-lined sheepskin jacket with its wide collar. Her mustard-yellow woollen mini-dress fitted her snugly. She was wearing white knee-length boots. Tasteful jewellery adorned her neck and wrists. Sally wiggled by one or two of the chaps onto the upholstered settee at the back of the table. She tossed her hair and, as usual when she arrived said, "Can I get some drinks?"

She got a five pound note from the purse kept in her colourful tapestry handbag.

"Here, let me." Dylan took the note from her.

"Thanks. I'll have my usual Martini please," said Sally. Dylan checked everyone else wanted their usual and got to the bar as Norman arrived, a bit breathless as usual. Norman was always a bit later than the others as he was still working. He helped Dylan carry the drinks.

"Cheers," everyone said. "Anyone seen Tom?" someone asked. They hadn't. "Adrian won't be coming tonight either, he was saying last week."

"You seem a bit preoccupied Bruce. Everything all right?" asked Rob. Bruce hadn't said much so far. "I'm fine, thanks Rob," he said.

"We'd better have a practice game, hadn't we?" said Fred. "It's the last chance we'll get before playing the *Bull* crowd next week." They sorted themselves out into two friendly teams and played darts for an hour. Raymond's team just beat Sally's. She was still throwing some good arrows.

Tom rushed in, a bit breathless. "Just called in to say I'm sorry I couldn't make it tonight. Spot of bother with my old Mum's washing machine. I've had to try and fix it for her. I think I've done it. Is it on for next week? I should be here then. Yes, thanks, I'll just have a half." As an afterthought he said, "Lovely big moon out there. Lights everything up. It's a real frost already though."

As Tom was finishing his half a pint, one by one the friends stood up to say their goodbyes and began to leave. See you next week," they were saying. It was about 9.30.

As usual, almost as a ritual, somebody asked Sally if she would like to be walked home. It's dark out there, they said. As always, Sally declined with thanks. She was an independent girl. In fact, after all these years, nobody appeared to know much about Sally, other than she was enjoyable company and could play a good game of darts.

Fred left first, from the door at the side of the pub. Raymond and Janet and then Rob left by the other door to the car park. Sally left by the side door, followed by Dylan, then Bruce a few minutes later. Tom finished his half pint, while he and Jim had a brief chat about the match next week. They left together. Norman decided, as he so often did, that he was in no rush to leave, bought himself another pint of bitter and sat in his usual comfortable chair by the fire.

◆ ◆ ◆

Bruce arrived home and opened the front door with his key. Jennifer heard him and came into the hall. "You look perished," she said. "Come and get warm. Would you like a hot drink or something?" She always worried about Bruce. Things hadn't been easy but she would be lost without him. The last thing she wanted was for him to get pneumonia or something, on top of everything else.

"Yes, there's going to be a hard frost but there's a nice big moon," he said. "Maybe some cocoa or something."

They sat by the gas fire with their cocoas. Joe had barely stirred. Jennifer asked if it had been a good evening. He told her about the darts friendly game in preparation for next week's match. They chatted for a while, then went to bed.

Bruce was restless and couldn't sleep. He decided that maybe two pints in an evening, at his age, was a bit too much. Eventually he dropped off.

CHAPTER 5

Constable Stevens was none too pleased with his lot that Friday morning. Due to some mis-match in numbers he had been instructed to do a quick turnround from his late duty on Thursday to early morning on Friday. That meant an 0545 start. He was given Millwood town centre beat. He knew the ice on the roads and pavements would hang around most of the day.

It was now about 0945. He was walking generally in the direction of the Nick, thinking of his break and the egg and bacon sandwiches waiting in his bag. Even with big police issue boots, he walked carefully, avoiding the worst ice patches.

Turning a corner, he saw a group of people outside the *George and Dragon*. An old lady had, despite everything, decided to do her shopping at Tesco's. She always did, at that time on Fridays. "Before the crowds," she would say. Leaving

Tesco's with her full bag and walking by the pub, she inevitably slipped on an ice patch. Now she lay on the ground saying her side hurt, unable to get up. The landlord, Geoffrey, had been cleaning tables in the bar and witnessed the whole thing from a window. He had called an ambulance and taken a blanket out.

PC Stevens used his radio to ask for a check on how long the ambulance would be. "It'll be a while. They're busy with RTAs everywhere. Probably at least 30 minutes, they say." That's going to keep me tied up for a time, he thought.

◆ ◆ ◆

Detective Sergeant Harris parked his car and called into Divisional Control to report himself back from leave and on duty.

"Sounds busy," he said. The two PCs in the room were dealing with the usual spate of early morning crime reports and local traffic problems caused by the ice. Resources were stretched. Chattering away to itself on low volume was a loudspeaker which was the feed from the Force Control radio. It sometimes helped to know the big picture.

"Yes, accidents all over the place. Traffic Division are pushed. And there's a pile up on the motorway. People taking tumbles on icy pavements. The Siberian weather's come early this year. It's taken folk by surprise."

Harris climbed the stairs to the CID office. Taylor and DC Harlow arrived together a few minutes later. "Morning Sarge." "Morning all. Lovely morning," said Harris, sounding particularly cheery despite having returned from his two days' leave.

"Did it go well?" asked Taylor. "Houses, I mean."

"I think so. We'll have to see," Harris smiled at the thought. "How about you two? Have you nabbed any Mister Bigs in the thieving world yet? Oh, yes, and how's your elbow, Richard?" he added.

"Not too bad now, thanks. We're working on the case but it's a bit tricky at the moment."

"Okay, as soon as the DI gets here I want to talk to him about that drugs thing in Millwood and we can see what he wants to do with your case as well."

◆ ◆ ◆

Joe stood at the door, clearly eager for his walk. It was a bright sunny morning. The early frost had covered trees and bushes in a beautiful sparkling way.

As usual, Jennifer was fussing about Bruce.

"I've remembered to put my Shetland jumper on and I've got my scarf and woolly hat. And gloves. And I'll try not to forget the paper this morning," Bruce said, fingering some coins in his trouser pocket.

As Bruce and Joe walked steadily through the wood, there wasn't much frost on the ground, it was all on the tree tops. Their breath came out as white plumes. The place seemed even more still and quiet than usual.

Yesterday, Bruce had noticed the wide patch of ash and partly burned sticks which had been the remains of Wednesday's bonfire. He had been pleased no real damage had been caused. Just a bit of scorching of nearby bushes which didn't really matter. Nothing had changed today.

"Joe," called Bruce. Joe had wandered off as usual to do some sniffing but had been gone longer than usual.

"Joe," he called a bit louder. Joe barked. That was unusual. Joe seldom barked these days. He must have found something interesting. The sound came from some distance away, down the overgrown path to the right which led to the gap in the fence. Joe never ran off but Bruce didn't want to risk him getting through that gap.

Bruce walked as quickly as he could along

the little path, brushing aside the encroaching branches. A few yards before getting to the fence, Joe was standing there. He looked at Bruce, then looked again at what he had found. He lowered his head and sniffed.

Joe was looking at a woman lying face down on the ground. Bruce's ambulance instincts kicked in and he bent forward to see if he could help, thinking of first aid, resuscitation.

He froze. In seconds he knew he couldn't help. This woman was dead. Her face was buried in a patch of brambles. Her left arm was splayed out at an unnatural angle. He couldn't see her right arm as it was concealed entirely under her body. Her sheepskin coat was somehow twisted around her, revealing a yellow dress which had partially ridden up, revealing her right thigh up to her buttock. Her legs, in black tights and high white boots, were splayed across the path.

There was something about this dead woman. Bruce remained frozen to the spot, wide-eyed. He felt as though his insides were melting and draining from his body. His heart started pounding and it seemed louder than the passing diesel engine over beyond the far side of the wood. The pulsing was almost painful in his head.

Seconds which felt like minutes went by. Bit by bit, he tried to think. He stood and then bent down again, reached out and pulled the hem of the yellow dress down a bit.

Instinctively he said, "Joe, come here." He clipped Joe's lead to his collar. Time stood still, it seemed. Everything he could see was through a pounding mist.

Then it hit him. It was that old silly thought he once had about how he would feel if he found a dead body. Now it had happened. He was wishing with all his might that it hadn't. He wished he wasn't there. He fought against a rising emotion, tears welling up. He forced them back. The image of the woman wearing a sheepskin coat, yellow dress and white boots somehow seemed familiar. The moment went in a flash but then returned more persistently. He slowly became aware of who that dead woman was. His brain was not functioning properly but a terrible, terrible thought emerged and became more persistent.

He couldn't just stand there. He looked around and saw nobody. He hardly ever saw anybody in the wood. He must think of one thing at a time. That was it. He was the only one who knew about this. Better report it, get help. Nothing else to do. Phone box. He tugged Joe who was a bit reluctant and still curious about his clever find. "Come on Joe, good boy, let's be quick."

Unthinking instinct took them back along the

little path towards the clearing where the bonfire had been and on to the iron gate into Beech Street. Reflecting on his actions later, Bruce would wonder why on earth he hadn't taken the shortcut to the town centre where there were people and shops. Of course, he never had reason to know there had even been a policeman just a hundred yards away looking after an old lady who had slipped on the ice. That would have been much quicker.

On the other hand there was no hurry, not really.

Bruce walked as quickly as he could, trying to run. Joe wondered why. Bruce's mind was reminding him he knew how the 999 system worked but he had to force himself to remember he didn't need any money for that. The image from the other day flashed into his head, of the smashed glass in the phone box. Had the phone been vandalised? Should he knock on someone's door and ask to use their phone? Probably they're all at work. Maybe take ages to find someone in. Quicker to keep going. He was breathing heavily, his and Joe's breath coming in large white clouds in the frosty air. It's not far. Just around the corner.

Turning right at the end of Beech Street into Forest Road they arrived at the phone box. Joe followed Bruce into the tight space and wondered what this strange behaviour was all about. The door closed.

Bruce lifted the receiver, removed a glove and when he had stopped his finger trembling, he dialled 9...9...9. He seemed to be floating outside himself and watching what he was doing from several feet away. The pounding in his head was slowing down.

Almost instantly a sharp female voice said into his ear, "Emergency, which service do you require?" That brought him down to earth a bit. He had forgotten there would be that stage. It made him hesitate for a moment. Ambulance? No. No point in that. Don't want to waste their time. Not today.

"Police, er, please," he said.

There were a few clicks and a ringing tone which went on, it seemed to him, for far too long. Eventually, after only about four rings, there was another click.

A slightly distant voice, male this time and sounding quite casual, said, "Police, can I help you?"

◆ ◆ ◆

The Inspector in charge of the Force Control Room this morning knew it would be busy. They were still short staffed and only five of the six positions in front of him were occupied. The Sergeant might have to step in.

The early frost was finding people unprepared. Vehicles were sliding and engines were boiling up. As the morning progressed, calls were coming in about accidents and one of the civilian control assistants was dealing with little else but breakdowns on the motorway.

Two officers sat at the middle desks, despatching mobiles by radio from job to job as soon as possible, keeping track of where they all were. Inevitably there would be delays this morning, especially as an early call to the motorway had turned out to be a major incident completely closing the southbound carriageway.

At the right hand radio position was PC Simon Baker. On his right was the other civilian control assistant, Donald Ross. Donald was a young man who had been working in the control room for almost two years. He enjoyed the job but knew it could only be temporary as there was no career ladder to climb. His work was efficient enough, albeit with a slightly casual approach. He didn't have the years or the police experience to understand some of the public's needs and emotions. But he was learning and could efficiently take messages.

A red light began pulsing on each desk and a soft persistent beep sounded around the room.

There was an unwritten rule that a 999 call must be answered within four or five pulses, preferably less. Everyone was busy.

Donald abruptly finished his current call to a Division and pressed down the switch under the pulsing light. The beeping noise stopped and, imperceptibly, the voice recorder in the drawer below his desk clicked.

"Police, can I help you?" Donald said. He could just make out the sound of someone breathing fast. That wasn't unusual. People often ran to make an emergency call, he supposed.

He repeated, "Can I help you? Take your time. What's happened?"

Bruce spoke. "There's a dead body," he said, croaking a bit. "In the wood."

Such a message wasn't unknown in the Control Room but not frequently, thank goodness, Donald was thinking. There's always the possibility of a hoax of course. But maybe not at that time on a Friday morning, kids being at school.

"Okay, Sir, which wood?" asked Donald.

"I'm sure she's dead ... not moving ...," Bruce paused.

"What's your name?" asked Donald.

Instinctively, control room staff become aware of a non-routine call going on. Next to

Donald, Simon Baker had just completed directing a traffic car to yet another road accident. Whenever there was such a spare moment he would press a switch to listen in to any current 999 call. It helped to speed things up if he could get a response on the way while the caller was still reporting an incident.

He switched into Donald's call, heard him ask for the caller's name and then attracted Donald's attention. "Where?" he said quietly. He needed a location.

Bruce said, "I ...," just as a tremendously loud, screaming noise hit both Donald's and PC Baker's ear drums. They instantly moved their earpieces from their ears. The noise lasted just 5 or 6 seconds.

"What was that?" asked Donald.

"It was the jet planes flying over. Training," said Bruce who had sounded as though he was gently sobbing but now regaining a little composure, probably helped by the startling noise almost overhead.

"That's okay then, Sir," said Donald. "Would you tell me where you are please?"

"I ... I'm in the phone box. Forest Road. It's in the woods off Beech Street," Bruce said, then realising that wasn't enough, "Millwood."

PC Baker nodded and called up a West Division area car which was a couple of miles away. He then pressed the switch for the direct line to West Division Control. "Thanks. Just heard it on the radio. Have you got details yet?"

"Listen, Sir, I didn't get your name," Donald said.

"Morgan. Bruce Morgan."

"Where do you live?" asked Donald. Bruce told him and went quiet. Bruce had done all he could. He felt drained and didn't know what to do now. He was suddenly emotional again. That terrible thought ... Sally ... His knees became weak, he let go of the receiver and he sank to the floor of the kiosk putting an arm around Joe's neck. He cried. Joe licked his face.

Donald said that help was on the way and that Mr. Morgan should remain where he was. Realising Bruce had gone he disconnected and passed on the final details to West Division.

The sergeant and constable in the area car found Bruce and Joe in the telephone kiosk a few minutes later.

CHAPTER 6

Constable Stevens waited with the old lady outside the George and Dragon until the ambulance arrived. Both she and he were cold. He had used his greatcoat to help keep her warm. He was glad when the ambulance attendant brought out blankets and he could retrieve his coat. After a quick examination, the attendant said it was a typical fractured neck of femur. To the old lady he had added, "You won't be dancing on ice again for a bit, love." They carefully got her onto a scoop stretcher, into the ambulance and on the way to hospital.

Over an hour had gone by, dealing with this one incident. PC Stevens was once again walking back towards the Nick with visions of his sandwiches and steaming mugs of tea. He became aware there was something going on. He turned up the volume on his pocket radio. A body found in Millwood. Control called him. "PC 1075 go to Beech Street. Report of a body found in the wood. Area car in attendance. Panda and CID on the way, over." "Roger, received, on my way, over," he replied, turned on his heels and walked as quickly as possible, back past the pub to Beech Street. Two police cars with blue lights flashing were parked just around the corner from the phone box.

"You'll need to show us where you found the, er, body," the sergeant who was one of the crew of the area car was saying to Bruce. He had been helped out of the phone box and was still firmly gripping Joe's lead. He was leaning against the wall of a house looking exhausted and drained. His orange woolly hat was askew. His missing glove had been retrieved from the floor of the kiosk. With an effort, without saying anything, he began to walk, still holding Joe's lead, along Beech Street, accompanied by the two policemen. The others followed, driving the cars to the end of the street.

The sergeant said to one of the constables, "Stay here at the gate. Nobody to enter the wood. CID are on their way."

"Yes, Sarge."

"Stevens, you know this beat. You'd better come with us." Bruce and the three officers went into the wood. They got to the clearing where the bonfire had been.

Bruce was now really feeling a kind of delayed shock. He stopped walking and pointed to the almost invisible path. "Down there," he said in a whispered croak.

"Right," the sergeant said to the constable, "take Mr Morgan back and put him and the dog in your panda and stay with him until CID get here. Okay?"

"Right, Sarge." He guided Bruce and Joe back to the street and sat them in the back of the car. The constable sat in the driver's seat, instantly discovering that he didn't quite know what to say to someone who had just found a body. He thought he should say nothing in case he fell foul of some procedure. Bruce sat in silence.

To PC Stevens, who had now forgotten all about his sandwiches, the sergeant said, "Come on, we'd better go and find this body."

◆ ◆ ◆

Like PC Stevens, DS Harris also heard the radioed instructions going out about a body in Millwood. He was just about to speak when the phone on DI Merton's desk rang. Merton answered it, listened for a short while, scribbled some notes and said, "Right, we're on it. Usual instructions. No big coppers' boots anywhere near it. Understood? Oh and a few uniform around to keep the ghouls out." He put the receiver down.

"We've got a body found in Millwood," he said. He was thinking they'd got some proper action at last.

Harris was already getting his coat on. "Yeah, just picked it up."

DI Merton was heading for the door. "Taylor, you're with us. Harwood, hold the fort."

"Sir," said Harwood. He was thinking dark thoughts about being left behind but he realised they could hardly leave Taylor holding the fort on a day like today. He had been given that responsibility!

The Rover weaved through the traffic, arriving in Beech Street about ten minutes after Bruce and Joe had been put into the panda car. The constable at the gate updated them.

A few local people had gathered, mostly standing on the pavement near Tallows' brown gates, quietly watching the activity across the road. At the house next to the gates the yellowing curtain was pulled back and a face appeared, looking out for a minute or two. Some of the observers were wondering if it was all to do with a drugs raid, maybe. Mrs. Robertson was there, convinced that was indeed the case and thinking how important her part in the investigation must have been. She was excitedly telling her neighbours about how helpful she had been to the detectives.

DI Merton opened the panda door and crouched down on the pavement to speak to Bruce. He could quickly see that Bruce was something of a nervous wreck. Understandable, he thought. "Hello, sir," he said gently. "You've had a bit of a shock, I guess. What happened?"

Bruce tried to explain but all he could mumble was something about walking the dog.

Merton summoned up his friendliest tone and said, "Right oh. No worries. What we'll do is take you home. Have a rest and one of us will come round later to take a statement. Will that be alright?"

As he was hearing this, Bruce's eyes were widening. "But … but … but …," he was trying to say something. He put has hand out to grasp Merton's sleeve.

"It's okay old chap, we'll see you later. Don't worry. We've got your address." He told the constable at the wheel, "33 Lyndon Avenue. Make sure he's alright."

"Right Sir," said the constable, starting the engine. He skilfully did a u-turn and drove off.

Watching the car depart, DI Merton said, "Thank goodness he's switched his bloody blue light off."

To Harris and Taylor he said, "Let's go and see what we've got."

❖ ❖ ❖

Jennifer never worried if Bruce was later than usual getting home. Once in a while he would bump into someone he knew, maybe one of his Thursday Club mates. If the *George and Dragon* had opened they might go in for a drink. Or more likely at a café in town or Tesco's coffee shop.

She thought that must have happened today. That is until there was a knock on the front door. There was Bruce looking rather strange, holding Joe by the lead and accompanied by a policeman.

"Oh, what on earth has happened?" Jennifer could see that Bruce had had a shock. He didn't look right at all. She scurried around, helping him out of his overcoat, taking Joe's lead off him, getting Bruce sat down in his chair, thinking about making his coffee, asking him what had happened several times.

The policeman had come in. "Don't worry, Madam. Your husband has had a bit of a shock this morning." He explained the bare outline of what had happened, as far as he knew it. "He's done a good job, done his public duty. He just needs a bit of time to come to terms with it. A bit of rest. Someone will come later on to take a statement. That's all. I'll leave you to it for now. Alright?"

Jennifer nodded, trying to take it all in. "Thank you very much for bringing them home." She saw the constable to the door.

She knelt down by his chair and held Bruce's hand. He suddenly leaned forward and hugged her tightly. She thought he seemed like a frightened little boy.

"It's all right, you're home now. I'm here," she said. Somehow, she was thinking, this seems to be the culmination of lots of small things. She remembered all the times since he had retired when he had seemed sad, forgetful, morose, anxious. It wasn't the first time she thought that maybe he should see the doctor about it. All this seems to have affected him really badly.

Joe looked on questioningly, then put his head on Bruce's lap as usual. Bruce stroked him.

"Drink your coffee. Do you want something to eat?"

Bruce shook his head. He sat back and closed his eyes. His head was still spinning but gradually, while he was resting, the jumble of thoughts were gradually putting themselves into some order.

Jennifer left him to rest and went into the kitchen where the transistor radio was on and the local radio station was quietly talking to itself. She turned up the volume. Breaking news, they were saying rather breathlessly. Body found in woods at Millwood. Was it murder? Investigation under way ...

◆ ◆ ◆

The sergeant and PC Stevens pushed cautiously through the bushes along the little path until they saw the bundle of sheepskin and yellow clothing lying to one side, its whitebooted legs spread across the path. Neither officer needed telling about avoiding contamination of a crime scene. It was all part of basic training. But no crime scene was ever quite as it looked in the demonstrations at training school. The sergeant came to a quick decision. He told PC Stevens to circle as widely as possible through the trees to get past the body and then stand near, not too near, the jagged gap that he could see in the fence. He had no idea what was on the other side but he didn't want any surprise visitors. Nor did he want evidence destroying. "That'll do. Just there," he told Stevens who then stood motionless.

Knowing it was a chance in a million but knowing it was his duty, the sergeant stepped forward gingerly, wanting to make sure there was no chance the victim was still alive. He wouldn't want any mistake like that on his conscience. He picked up a rigid stick and used it to carefully move aside the brambles which were covering the left side of her face. What he saw convinced him that this body was indeed deceased.

The sergeant carefully walked back a short way along the path. He reported the position by radio and said that, if an ambulance had been called, it could be stood down.

He and PC Stevens stood silently, on guard, waiting for CID to arrive.

As PC Stevens stood there, he reflected that Mr Morgan must have been finding the body at just about the same time as he, Stevens, was attending to that old lady, little more than a hundred yards away, by the *George and Dragon*, the back of which could be seen. As he stood there facing the sergeant, with the body lying between them, he no longer felt hungry.

◆ ◆ ◆

Acting Chief Inspector Johnson was currently in charge of West Division. He was keen to be doing the right thing. You never knew if CID might need house to house inquiries. That kind of thing. He brought several more officers into Millwood, mostly into Beech Street in case they were needed but sent one PC to stand guarding the entrance to the path which led down the side of the *George and Dragon*. The hapless PC was fully expecting to have to stand there for much of the rest of the day, right next to the open kitchen window of the pub where they were in full swing cooking pub grub. Somebody did take pity on him and brought him a mug of tea.

◆ ◆ ◆

"Pathologist, forensics," said DI Merton as soon as he arrived and stood next to the sergeant viewing the scene. DS Harris was on to his pocket radio. He learned that a pathologist and a forensics team were both well on their way.

Taylor stood quietly behind them, slightly apprehensive, looking at the body and wondering if she really ought to have wished to be involved in a serious case. She took a few deep breaths. It would be alright, she told herself.

The sergeant thought he should mention what he had done. "The side of her face is bashed in. Thought I ought to check for life, Sir," he added.

Merton was running a basic checklist through his mind and was speaking it out loud. "Thanks sergeant. So it does look like murder. The ground's still frost hard. Not likely to see any marks on the ground. Murder weapon? Anybody see anything likely? If her head's bashed in there must be something heavy enough. Blood on it. Could still be around. Motive? Too early for that. Unless she's a prostitute. Any in Millwood? We'll see. Who is she anyway? Can't do much till forensics and the Doc get here."

"Hope it's old whatshisname .. Franklyn. He's an old codger but he talks in our language. Some of these young ones … all science and no sense," he was muttering.

"Sir," PC Stevens called across and was pointing over to his right, "there's something possible just there. It's grey fence rail. Looks like a broken part of this fence." Merton glanced at DS Harris who carefully walked around to where PC Stevens was pointing. "We meet again," he said to the constable.

There was clearly a sizeable piece of timber, a similar grey colour to the fence, lying in a patch of long grass a few yards from the body, between two trees, where it had been tossed away. "Yeah, I bet that's it," he said.

◆ ◆ ◆

Beech Street was getting busy.

Three more constables had arrived and the group of them were standing at the iron gate. A white van parked nearby. Two men got out, went to the rear doors and donned white plastic suits, then carried heavy cases into the wood. One had an impressive looking camera around his neck. A big two-tone grey and black Humber arrived and parked rather untidily right next to the iron gate. An older, white haired man in a suit and tie stepped out. He was wearing a heavy overcoat and carrying a black case. He and one of the constables entered the wood.

It was now about 12.45. A white van with 'Radio Easterby' splashed in red letters on the side sped down the street. It stopped and a white dish aerial slowly emerged from its roof. A young man with a microphone began to dash about among those watching. He was muttering something about the one o'clock news. He completely confused a Mrs. Robertson when he mentioned a body being found. She had convinced herself that a drugs raid was going on.

An anonymous black van slipped into the street and parked a little further away. Two men waited patiently inside.

A little later and almost unnoticed by the crowd on the opposite side of the street, a woman was pushing herself with some difficulty in an old squeaking wheelchair. She had emerged from the entry at number 66, about a dozen doors away from the iron railings. She determinedly pushed herself slowly and painfully towards the group of constables. She stopped next to them.

"Can I help you, Madam?" said one.

"What's happening?" she said.

"We don't really know very much ourselves, yet."

"On the news just now it said a body had been found," the woman said.

"I believe that's correct."

She looked at him. "Thank you." She quickly looked away. Her grey hair was untidy, her face was grey and grim. She spun her chair around and pushed herself back the way she had come. Tears began to flood down her face. Her deep uncontrollable sobs were unseen. She pushed herself, barely noticed by anyone, into her entry.

CHAPTER 7

The plastic-suited forensics guys were going over everything, photographing everything and making a search of the wider area. That wasn't easy because of all the brambles and other undergrowth.

"There's that piece of timber especially. I want to take a look at that as soon as you're done with it," DI Merton was saying, "and that gap in the fence and whatever is beyond it might be useful. Doubt whether there's much on the ground. Very hard frost."

"Well, here's your lump of timber," one of the plastic-suited guys said through his mask, showing it to Merton. It had been placed in a plastic evidence bag. "Can't find any prints but you wouldn't expect to on an old piece of wood. It will have to go to the lab to have that blood checked." Merton looked closely at the reddish-brown staining at one end. "Not much doubt this is what did the damage."

"What did what damage?" Dr. Franklyn, the pathologist, had bustled down the path onto the scene.

"Good to see you, Doc.," said Merton, "It's been a while. Glad it's you on this one."

"Let's take a look at that. So you think that did the damage to her, do you? Let's see," Franklyn took a cursory glance. "A bit rotten, it's a wonder it didn't break. Preservative, I suppose."

He glanced at the body, noting that the face was invisibly buried in the brambles, the left arm sticking out, the right arm tucked completely underneath.

"You've got your snaps have you?" The other forensics guy with the camera nodded. "Have you got something to put down over those brambles, we don't want to cause more damage to her face to complicate things. Bloody devils those thorns. Then we'll roll her over and see what's what."

Taylor stepped back two paces as she watched them firmly grasp the woman's left arm, shoulder and leg and roll her onto her back.

"Well," said Dr. Franklyn, "It certainly looks as though your lump of wood might have done the trick." Everyone was looking at the mass of dried blood and matted hair on the left side of her face. "Eye socket and cheek bone gone by the looks of it. A lot of bleeding. It knocked her brain for six and she probably bled out from the main artery that goes up the side of the face. A mighty blow that was."

Franklyn was in his stride. "I'll have to do the measurements but that bit of wood looks like the culprit. The blow probably spun her around which is why she was face down. Might have bumped that tree as well." There was a bruise in the centre of her forehead.

DI Merton was about to speak when Franklyn anticipated him. "Time, you want, I suppose. Difficult with this frost. Changes things, doesn't it? Best guess - yesterday evening before midnight. Doesn't look as if she's been interfered with. Tights still intact. Oh yes, and you'll want the gory bits like stomach contents as well, won't you? We'll do all that at the PM tomorrow. Two o'clock. You can shift her there now. I've done."

With that he was gone. He was soon followed by the forensics guys.

The scene was now very different. The woman was now on her back. She had a face, albeit a badly damaged one. Most of her hair was matted with blood. She was tightly clutching a handbag in her right hand. It was one of those colourful, patterned, tapestry bags. Even though she had been lying on it, the clasp was undone. The bag hadn't been spotted before as it had been completely underneath her.

"Well, somebody's got to do it," said Merton. He crouched down by the body and with some force prized the two frozen fingers open so he could retrieve the bag. He grabbed a nearby stick, probably the same one the sergeant had used to move the brambles, and used it to carefully lift the bag.

"Taylor!" called Merton. Taylor didn't speak but stepped closer.

"Get an evidence bag, put this on it, open it without touching anything more than you have to and see what's inside."

From the moment Taylor had known she was to be seconded to the CID she was aware she had to be prepared for such things. For detectives, she had thought, evidence bags were a kind of badge of office. From her first day in CID she had made sure she had several different sizes with her, in her shoulder bag. She found the largest one, spreading it on the hard ground. She was now very close to a dead body for the first time in her life but, with something to do, she felt a lot better.

DI Merton lowered the handbag onto the plastic. "There's not really going to be any prints on it. But we'll be careful."

"Sir," Taylor finally spoke and gingerly pulled the cold bag open to reveal the contents. The obvious things were a slim brown diary with a pencil fastened by loops to the spine, a small, folded handkerchief, a compact, a lipstick and not much else apart from a one pound note and some loose coins.

DI Merton was watching this and deciding that Taylor was doing a good job. "There won't be any prints or anything like that worth having, so hang onto the bag and bring it with you. Right, let's get the body moved."

The sergeant made a radio call to a constable at the gate who walked down the street to the anonymous black van and spoke to the driver. It drove nearer the gate, a trolley was taken out of the back and the two men and the constable wheeled the trolley into the wood.

◆ ◆ ◆

An hour later there was nothing more to see. Beech Street emptied apart from a panda car and two constables who were detailed to remain at the gate, "to reassure the public," they had been told. The public had gradually dispersed. The action was over.

The constable guarding the path by the pub

had, to his surprise, been told to resume his normal beat duties.

Having a final look around, DI Merton had said, "It's as though nothing has happened. Now we've got to put things together and see where it leads us." The one thing running through his mind was that he wanted to get this one tied up quickly and efficiently. Somehow, he thought it could be. If not it would involve the Superintendent from HQ coming over and getting his mitts all over it. To be avoided, he decided. But then, he always did.

"Right. First things first. PC Stevens, you're the beat man around here I gather. Do you happen to know when that pub closes?"

PC Stevens replied that he was sure the *George and Dragon* usually closed at 1400 hours but stayed open all day on Fridays and the weekend. "Good show," said Merton. He and DS Harris and Taylor returned to the Rover in Beech Street. Merton drove around to the car park of the *George and Dragon*.

The sergeant told PC Stevens to go to get his break. Better late than never. PC Stevens now realised he was very hungry.

◆ ◆ ◆

At lunchtimes on Fridays, the *George and*

Dragon is busy with many elderly locals enjoying their weekly lunchtime 'OAP Specials'. There is an inevitable good natured early scrap for tables. So it was those happy pensioners who were leaving now, around two o'clock, as Merton Harris and Taylor arrived. They had a choice of tables and chose one in a quiet alcove.

It wasn't typical of DI Merton but today he said, "What are you having?" His was a pint and the others had soft drinks. Merton also ordered himself a pasty. Harris and Taylor decided on sandwiches. Taylor still hadn't decided whether or not it was a good idea to bring her own packed lunch to work.

The few remaining locals, mostly at the bar, exchanged knowing glances. After all, the news of the body in the wood had quickly become common knowledge in the town.

DI Merton said, "We've got a lot to do so we won't take long over this. Basically, who is she? That's top priority. Then who did it and why. We're pretty sure we know how."

Harris hadn't said a great deal for most of the morning. He had somehow felt that what had happened, the terrible scene he had witnessed, had played with his head. Of course, he was fairly used to similar scenes as part of the job. He found that he was contrasting all that with the previous two days of leave which had been so enjoyable; house hunting with Susan and choosing the one in which they would live happy lives together.

He said, "How about the diary from her handbag? There might be a clue in there."

"Yes, take a look. Should be something." Merton tucked into his pasty.

Taylor took the diary from the handbag and gave it to Harris.

Almost immediately, Harris had turned to the page at the beginning of the diary. It was, as expected, to record the owner's name and address.

"Here it is. She's Sally Weston. Address 66 Beech Street, Millwood."

"That's the easy bit done then," said Merton. "What about the handbag itself?"

Taylor took on the task of searching the handbag. "Well, there's not much. Compact, lipstick, handkerchief, a pound note, a few coins ... you'd think she'd have a purse. There's a Yale key on a plain ring. Then, in an inside pocket a couple of what look like membership cards. The Starlight Club and the Palais de Dance. One in Lupton and the Palais in Market Easterby. I know that place well - gets lively on a Saturday night." She was recalling memorable Saturday night duties crewing the GP van, in the town centre.

DI Merton said, "Hang on. I've been assuming she's a good time girl but without much money to go with it." He had a sudden thought. "How old do you reckon she is? I'm calling her a girl. Surely she's at least middle-age. Difficult to tell from what we've seen of her so far. Not too much of her face." The others didn't venture a guess.

DS Harris said, "Here's yesterday's date in her diary. There's a circle in blue ink around the date, 6th November. Then, looking through, there's the same circle around every first Thursday of the month. There's not a lot more in it. Just a few things like a dentist appointment. Oh, and three or four showing hospital appointments. Easterby General Hospital by the looks of it, together with a name. Margaret, it looks like."

"Right," DI Merton said, standing up. He had just finished his pasty. "We've got a few bits. Let's go and get more." He was on his way to the door.

Taylor hurriedly swept up the items on the table and put them back in the bag. She looked at her half emptied glass and the remains of her sandwich. Getting used to the strange ways of CID was very necessary.

They sat in the Rover. DI Merton said, "Taylor, you're with me. We're going to break the news to the family if there is one and see what we can discover at her address. What was it, 66 Beech Street?" DS Harris confirmed it was. "There's a phone number as well."

He continued, "Sergeant Harris, pick up a panda and go and get the statement from the guy who called it in. Morgan, wasn't it? Best if there's two of you. He was in a bit of a state. Take it easy with him. See you back at the office later," he added.

They drove around, once again, into Beech Street where a panda car was parked by the iron gate. The sun was already low in the sky and it was getting colder. Nobody was about. The two constables emerged from the panda as they approached.

DI Merton asked if everything was quiet and they confirmed it was. "I don't think there's any need for you here any longer. We'll see what tomorrow brings. Whose is the panda?"

"It's my panda beat this afternoon, Sir. Or it was. PC O'Brien, Sir."

"Okay, PC O'Brien. Take DS Harris here to the address he'll give you and accompany him while he takes a statement. On the way, drop your colleague off at the Nick." They both looked relieved.

The panda set off.

"Right, Taylor. Where's number 66?"

CHAPTER 8

"This might not be too easy," said Merton to Taylor. "Are you okay?"

"Yes, I'm fine, Sir," said Taylor, recalling the two or three emotion-charged occasions when, in uniform, she had been involved in breaking bad news to relatives. She knew this would be rather different.

They noted that the dark curtains behind the front window of number 66 were drawn closed. There was no door bell. DI Merton rapped the brass knocker on the letterbox. He listened. Nothing happened so he rapped it again. A faint voice from beyond the door said, "It's open."

He pushed the door half open, revealing an almost dark front room. He called in through the darkness. "It's the police. Could we speak to you please?"

"Yes, come in."

They went in and accustomed their eyes to the gloom. The only dim light was coming from the back room through the short passage which linked the two. Much of the space in the front room was taken up with a substantial bed covered in a blue counterpane which was a bit untidy. There were two pillows on it together with some unfolded items of clothing. A small table was next to the head of the bed. It had on it an unlit lamp, a few books and an empty glass tumbler. A slight odour in the room led Taylor to assume that the cube of dark furniture next to the foot of the bed might be a commode. She recalled a similar scene from her old granny's downstairs room when Taylor had been a little girl. They could just make out a few pictures hanging around the walls. There appeared to be nothing else in that room other than a small electric heater which stood on the floor with a wire plugged into a socket on the wall. It was not switched on. It was cold.

Silhouetted in the light coming through the short passage was a woman sitting in a wheelchair.

"Sorry to have to trouble you, Madam," said DI Merton. "I am Detective Inspector Merton and this is Detective Constable Taylor." They showed their warrant cards but the woman wasn't really able to see them in the gloom.

She reversed the wheelchair into the back room. They followed her through the short passage.

"Shut the door. Keep the warm in. Sit down." the woman sounded tense.

This small room was identical in size to the one Taylor had seen at Mrs. Robertson's the other day. The woman manoeuvred her wheelchair into a place next to the gas fire. One of the three bars was lit. Merton and Taylor sat on a fairly comfortable settee. There was a small table, covered with a green gingham tablecloth, and two chairs. A low sideboard stood against the back wall. It had a few things on it including a black bakelite dial telephone. A small television and a radio set were on a table opposite the woman. Behind her there was a door which, they assumed, would reveal the stairs.

"I've been expecting you. It's about Sally, isn't it?" she blurted out, stemming a sob and putting a handkerchief to her eyes.

Taylor was sitting nearest the woman. She looked at her and saw the grey, tear-streaked face of someone who hadn't slept. She put her hand on her arm. She wanted to do more but wasn't sure if there might be a proper procedure for this.

DI Merton said, "No, it isn't good news for you,

I'm afraid. I'm very sorry. What do you know?"

The woman took a few moments to compose herself. She spoke quickly as though she wanted to get it all out before breaking down in tears again. "Sally didn't come home last night … I didn't know what to do … She's sometimes been quite late but she's never not come home … I was awake … didn't go to bed … I heard … on the news this morning … somehow knew it must be her … she's my sister, you see … my big sister … I don't know what I'll do …" The sobs came again.

Taylor thought this was as close to being someone in despair as she would ever see. She said gently, "What's your name?"

"Margaret."

"Margaret, do you think a cup of tea would help? Shall I get us one?"

Margaret nodded. Taylor went through the far door into the small kitchen, filled the electric kettle and found some mugs and tea bags. There was half a bottle of milk in the fridge but she noticed there was barely anything else in there. She sniffed the milk and it was just okay.

DI Merton, meanwhile, was asking Margaret if she felt up to telling him a bit about Sally. Margaret had composed herself a little and told him that Sally worked in the office at Armstrong's, the factory at the end of Forest Road which made cardboard boxes. She was 49 years old and Margaret was two years younger. Sally was dedicated to looking after Margaret but sometimes needed a break to get away and enjoy herself so she went out some evenings. She always went out on Thursdays because she belonged to a darts team. She was good at playing darts. Sometimes she went dancing on a Saturday night … about once a month … that's when she would sometimes come back a bit late.

"But she always came back …" Margaret broke down again. "Sorry … sorry …" she tried to say.

"It's quite alright, Margaret. We know it's very difficult to take in." Merton was saying as reassuringly as he could but knowing that nothing he could say would be adequate.

Taylor came in with three mugs of tea and a sugar bowl, all on a tray which she placed on the table.

There was a silence for a few minutes and then Margaret said, "I expect you are wondering why I'm like this." She went on. "It was a road accident. A few years after the war. 1950. We were young. Sally had only been married a year and they'd bought this old car. A Morris 10. We went for a spin one afternoon. Bill was driving of course and for some reason I sat in the front passenger seat. I think they were proud of their car and were showing it off to me. Wanted me to have a front seat view. Sally was in the back. There was this lorry …"

She paused, squeezed her eyes tight closed, as though trying to avoid re-living what had happened. "I'll never forget … sorry … the steering wheel went through Bill's chest. It was my spine. No seat belts then you see. It's just my legs I can't use. It could really have been a lot worse. Sally was in the back seat. Just broke her ankle. She's always felt so guilty she wasn't in front …" Again, Margaret's story petered out.

"What happened to her?" Margaret said, as though it had just at that moment occurred to her.

DI Merton had been thinking hard, still listening to Margaret's story. He told her, gently, that they were still trying to work that out but she had been found in the woods. Someone had attacked her. Margaret nodded.

Remembering the empty cupboards and fridge in the kitchen, Taylor said, Margaret, have you eaten anything? Is there anything you need? Is there anyone we can get in touch with for you? A neighbour?"

"My brother … our brother … Graham … lives in London. He's all there is. Our Mum's in a home. She doesn't know what goes on these days, thank goodness. Graham will be at work.

No, not eaten .. haven't felt like it. Sally always went to Tesco's on Fridays … she finished at work early on Fridays and got paid … she should be at Tesco's now …" There were more sobs.

Taylor whispered to Merton indicating there didn't seem to be any food to speak of in the house.

"Right," said Merton, clearly coming to some decisions. "Do you mind if I use your phone?"

He dialled the direct number of the CID office.

"West Division CID, DC Harlow speaking."

"Merton here, Harlow. How is it there?"

DC Harlow replied, "I've recorded a few jobs to get on with. I've monitored a bit of what's going on at Millwood. I guess it's going to be busy. Oh, and Detective Superintendent Briggs was on, earlier, wanting you to get in touch with him, Sir."

"I bet he does," thought Merton. "Now listen, Harlow, I want you to come over right away to 66 Beech Street. Taylor's here, she'll fill you in. When you're both done here you can get back to the office. We're all going to be finishing late today."

"I'll be on my way in a jiffy, Sir," said DC Harlow, now pleased to be involved.

DI Merton dialled another number. "Put me

through to Acting Chief Inspector Johnson, please." Then, turning his back on Margaret and speaking quietly, said "Archie, it's John Merton here. I stood your two PCs down in Beech Street. No need for them for the remainder of today and they were freezing. I've borrowed PC O'Brien to run around with my sergeant to get a statement."

"Yes," said Johnson, "they reported in. That's fine."

"Right, here's a meatier challenge for you," went on Merton. "Is there any chance you could rustle up the mobile police station tomorrow for a couple of days? Put it in Beech Street from, say 0800 tomorrow to 1600 Sunday, perhaps with a PC of yours with one or two of mine. Near the black iron railings at the end of the street. It's the weekend. People about. Give some reassurance and maybe a few might have information."

"Leave it with me, I'll organise it if I can," replied Johnson.

DI Merton replaced the receiver, turned to Margaret and told her that he would have to go now to get on with things and the police would do their very best.

He glanced at Taylor and then continued, telling Margaret that DC Taylor would stay for a while and that another officer would be joining her very soon. Between them, they'll nip to Tesco's and would get her something to eat. "That will make you feel a bit better," he reassured her. "They'll do whatever's possible to help, see if there's a neighbour who can stay with you and they'll get in touch with your brother."

"That understood, Taylor?" She acknowledged that it was.

"Oh, just one more thing for the moment, Margaret. Where did Sally play darts on Thursday evenings?" Margaret told him it was at the *George and Dragon*.

He held Margaret's hand, trying to give her a bit of strength for a moment, and was gone.

Taylor was feeling that she now knew what the phrase, 'being thrown in at the deep end' actually felt like and she hoped Richard Harlow would get here soon.

To Margaret she said, "My name is Carol. Would you like another cup of tea?"

◆ ◆ ◆

Jennifer stayed in the kitchen busying herself with preparing for dinner but not really thinking very carefully about what she was doing. It was all a bit upsetting. She was letting Bruce rest, knowing he needed some time to come to terms with what had happened that morning. It had clearly been a big shock.

In the sitting room, Joe was aware everything was not as it should be. It had been a strange morning, ending up having a ride in a car. That had not happened for a while. So Joe remained on watch at Bruce's side.

The thumping in Bruce's head had gradually subsided. It had been a nightmare of a morning which had seemed to go on forever. He knew he had been very upset and emotional. He thought he had probably made an exhibition of himself. Now, after an hour or so sitting and quietly stroking Joe, things were beginning to sort themselves out into a few clear images which were easier to handle, one by one. He was much calmer now that, finally, he had reconciled the two most persistent images. The one of Sally full of life at the Club, playing darts and of everything else he knew about her. The other image of that dreadful sight of the body he had seen that morning. They were both images of Sally.

To add to it all, he had been vaguely conscious of feeling guilty for having had that persistent thought about wondering what it would be like to find a dead body. That was probably something to do with the degree of emotion he had felt. By now he had admitted to himself that it was silly and irrelevant.

Joe pricked up his ears and almost immediately the front door bell rang. Bruce heard Jennifer answer it. He thought of getting up but decided to stay in his chair.

The introductions were efficient. "Mr. Morgan? Sorry to trouble you, Sir. I believe you were expecting us? I am Detective Sergeant Harris and this is PC O'Brien. Are you up to giving us a statement now? I know it's been a rather upsetting morning for you."

"Yes, yes, it's okay," Bruce said, a bit hesitantly.

Jennifer said, "Would you like a cup of tea ... or anything?"

"Thank you, Madam. Tea would be very nice."

When all were settled with cups of tea the process of compiling a statement began. DS Harris slowly and carefully obtained every detail, beginning with some information about Bruce and his background. Then from the moment Bruce had left home that morning with Joe, the exact route of his daily walk, Joe's unusual barking, right through to the difficult part of finding the body, to the moment he had made the 999 call. DS Harris carefully wrote it all down on the printed statement form. Bruce, his head now sorted out into a calmer state, was remembering it all quite clearly.

"There are just two more things I must ask," Harris said. "Did you touch the body at all, maybe checking to see if there was any life?"

"No. Perhaps I should have done something but no, there was no reason to." He then remembered, "I did pull her dress down a bit, to cover her leg. That's all."

"Thank you," said Harris. "Now, I have to ask this. When you were looking at the, er, body, did you by any chance recognise who it was?"

Bruce looked up, realising that a bit of his earlier upset was returning. He said, "I think so ... can't be quite sure ... couldn't see her face... but her yellow dress and her jacket ... yes, I'm sure it was Sally."

"How do ... sorry ... did, you know Sally?"

"Thursday Club ... the darts team ... met every Thursday ... been doing it for years ... *George and Dragon* ... miss her ...," Bruce's voice trailed into silence.

DS Harris was writing it all down.

"Now, we just need your signature on this please, Mr. Morgan. Bruce added a spidery signature and date to the form.

"Thank you. In due course you will almost certainly be needed to attend an inquest, at least," said Harris. "For now, I'd just like to thank you for doing your public service, calling us to report it. I'm really sorry it was such an upsetting experience for you. That should be it."

Bruce nodded. He felt exhausted again and sank back into his chair. He was hoping that was it. Goodbyes were said. Jennifer showed Sergeant Harris and PC O'Brien to the door.

"Thanks for that," Harris said to the panda driver. "It needs two present at these things really. You'll have to run me up to DHQ now, I'm afraid. The investigation begins."

❖ ❖ ❖

Jennifer drew the curtains. She said to Bruce, "Let's just sit for a while. I'll get dinner in a bit. Do you think it would be a good idea to have a glass of wine now, instead of leaving it till Sunday?"

For the first time that day, Bruce smiled, "Yes, dear, that's a good idea."

Joe settled down on the rug, curled up and snoozed.

❖ ❖ ❖

On his return to the CID office, Merton had phoned Detective Superintendent Briggs but had missed him. It was, after all, gone five o'clock on a Friday. That might have been a reprieve but not for long because Detective Superintendent Briggs phoned from his home just fifteen minutes later. "Evening John. Bring me up to speed on this murder will you? Where are we at?"

"Well, Sir. We got the call about a body found in some woods at Millwood just before eleven hundred hours this morning. Quick attendance by the area car. Sealed the scene. I arrived with Sergeant Harris and DC Taylor within half an hour. Forensics and pathology organised. The woman, around fifty years, had been bashed on the head. That looks like the cause of death but the PM is tomorrow at two. Identity established - she's local. We've gathered some information to start work on tomorrow. The four of us will be working up a plan shortly. Oh yes, Archie Johnson's organising the mobile police station for the weekend. For reassurance and we may pick up some information, Sir."

He had placed an emphasis on the words 'The four of us' hoping to indicate to Briggs how understaffed West Division CID was. The meeting at HQ the other day had not been about staffing.

Just then DS Harris came into the office, hung up his coat and sat at his desk, preparing to type up a report. He give the DI the thumbs up.

Briggs was telling DI Merton he would be keeping an eye on progress and a quick result was needed on this one. He would step in if the case looked as if it needed his additional authority. "If you need any more boots on the ground just say."

"Yes, Sir," Merton repeated. "We'll need some extra hands here in any case, if we're to keep on top of the routine stuff. I'll keep you informed. Good night, Sir".

"Right," he said to Harris, "The others should be on their way back. Call up Harlow and get them to bring a Chinese in. We must all be starving."

DS Harris did so but was thinking he would much rather be spending the evening with Susan, discussing the houses they had viewed. Yesterday seemed a long time ago.

While they waited, he and Merton discussed the day and confirmed they had learned that Sally had spent Thursday evening playing darts at the *George and Dragon*.

The door opened and DC Harlow and Taylor came in with a carrier bag. "Doesn't look much in there," said Merton.

"Well," said Taylor, "We've already eaten. Richard, er DC Harlow, arrived at Margaret's and then went out again to get a bit of shopping for her from Tesco's. When he got back we made something for all three of us because it made sense to keep Margaret company for a bit and it helped her to cheer up. If that could be possible," she added. "It was only an omelette and some beans with toast."

"Well done. How did she seem when you left? Just carry on telling us while I get into this sweet and sour."

DC Harlow left the talking to Taylor who obviously knew a lot more about the case.

Taylor said, "We got a neighbour - number 64, a Mrs Drummond - to help. They seemed to get on alright. She will help for a bit. The main thing is, I managed to track down the brother using Margaret's phone book. He is Graham Finlay. Margaret spoke to him on the phone. It was difficult obviously but I gathered he seemed to know that he needed to come to be with his sister. She really needs his help. He should be on his way from London as we speak. We washed up, told her someone would keep in regular touch and we left. It wasn't easy to leave her. She's a bit helpless. But Mrs. Drummond came round and sort of took charge. That should be okay for a bit."

"Graham Finlay?" DS Harris was holding a half-eaten spring roll in his fingers. "I thought it was Weston."

"No," said Taylor, "Sally was Weston because she had been married. Margaret and her brother are Finlay. I don't think I saw any rings on Sally's finger though, come to think of it." She briefly explained about the road accident and how terrible it had all been for the families.

"So Sally was a widow." DS Harris said and then, thinking about the cards they had found in her handbag and her darts playing at the *George and Dragon*, he added, "No rings. Probably a merry widow." Then he wished he hadn't said that.

The debris from the take-away was cleared away into a bin along the corridor.

Merton said, "We know quite a bit, like who the victim was and a fair bit about her. We know almost certainly how she died but the post mortem's tomorrow afternoon. So now we just need to find out who killed her and why. It was certainly no accident."

He went on, "We'll draw up an action list to get started on tomorrow. Then we can all go home. All suggestions welcome. Oh yes, Don't tell me someone's hoping to have the weekend off, let alone next week."

DC Harlow opened his mouth as if to speak but thought better of it and shut it again, especially having just been off for several days with his elbow. He'd just have to miss the match tomorrow.

"Taylor, you can use your expertise with the pinboard. Now you've tidied it up you can mess it up again. We haven't got any pictures from forensics yet but you can get a map up there to start with."

DS Harris said, "To state the obvious, she spent the evening in the pub playing darts. Who with? I think there's something called the Thursday Club. A darts team. Presumably the pub should be the first port of call."

"I think we'd all agree with that," said Merton. I'll knock up the landlord tomorrow morning. See what he knows. Mustn't forget the PM at two though. I've got to get into town for that. Who's coming with me? Not you Sergeant. Better have you on inquiries. Then there's the mobile police station. DC Harlow - you can man that from 0800 to 1200. There should be a PC with you if all goes to plan. We'll see if any of the locals want to talk to us about anything. I can't see any reason for door-to-door. We'll all meet up in Beech Street at 1200. Taylor can spend the afternoon there. DC Harlow can come with me to the PM. First time for everything, I'm guessing. That right, Harlow?"

Harlow nodded nervously. "Good man," said Merton.

"That's sorted then. What other lines have we got to follow? DS Harris has got to have something to do besides calling in for cups of tea at the mobile police station."

Taylor remembered that Sally had worked at

Armstrong's. She mentioned this and said, "She obviously didn't go in today so they will have wondered where she was, surely. They'll know by now of course. They'll still have her pay packet. Perhaps they phoned Margaret to check up. She didn't mention it."

"Agreed," said DI Merton. "And of course there's an outside chance there could have been something going on there, with the boss or whoever. Maybe the weekend's not the best time for that. We'll pursue that on Monday."

"Now," he went on. "Actually, Sergeant Harris, you can stick around Beech Street. Keep a general eye on things and call in on Margaret. Make her acquaintance. Ask how she's doing. That kind of thing. Reassure her we're pulling all the stops out. At the same time you can have a chat with her brother. It's a very long shot. But, you know, family feuds and all that. See if you can pick anything up. We need to rule that kind of thing out." As an afterthought he said, "Oh yes, and raise the question of identification will you? Probably going to have to be her brother."

"Right, Sir," said Harris. "I've just had another thought as well. Could this whole thing be random? Somebody lying in wait. Robbery? No - her bag was still with her. But, wait a minute. Taylor and I are supposed to be in the middle of investigating drug users in the wood, not that far away from where she was found. I was looking for a chance to have a word with you about that. Could they be involved, or maybe even witnessed it?"

"Yes," Merton said. "We'll add that possibility to the list. We're going to be busy. But, and it's a big but, have any of you given any thought to something which I think is probably at the heart of all this?"

They all wanted to hear DI Merton tell them what had obviously been missed, by the tone of his voice.

"I think we'll find the key to this if we can answer one question: Why there? She's lying across a narrow, almost invisible path, ten yards inside a dark wood near a gap in the fence to a dark footpath which runs about 100 yards to the street in the town centre. We're pretty sure she spent the evening at the pub. So she walks those 100 yards down that dark path. She goes through the narrow gap in the fence. Presumably, if she hadn't been clobbered on the head, she'd have carried on walking, probably another 300 yards or so - more than a quarter of a mile - through still more dark woods to the gate. Then it's just a short distance to home. By my reckoning, the distance from the *George and Dragon*, through the town square, along Forest Road and then down Beech Street can't be much further than that. So I just can't imagine why she would want to go through the wood as a shortcut to get home. Certainly not every Thursday. And not in November. I know she's 49 years old but she's still a comely lass. Would you do that, Taylor, even if there was a big, bright moon like last night?"

"Especially not if there was a moon like that. Creepy. No I wouldn't," said Taylor.

"So the question is - why was she there? It's not easy to get to, through the fence and all. I don't think her body was dragged from somewhere else - forensics might confirm or otherwise. There's no access for a vehicle. Somebody must have enticed her there. She doesn't sound like a prostitute, at 49. Or she accompanied someone she knew well enough. Through that narrow gap in the fence to her death."

With a sigh, DI Merton concluded, "That'll do for tonight. See you all in the morning."

CHAPTER 9

On the outskirts of Market Easterby, behind a small industrial estate, a group of anonymous brick buildings are the base for Traffic Division. Workshops, garages, offices and mess rooms form a u-shape around a large yard where there is a vehicle wash and, set separately, a small group of fuel pumps.

The seemingly unloved and little used Mobile Police Station is an almost permanent fixture in a corner of the yard. Years ago the Chief Constable and the Police Committee were persuaded that such an asset would prove useful at special events such as the County Show, gymkhanas and anywhere a police presence was needed. They had been less convinced of its value as a base for a murder investigations and the like. But the vision in the then Chief Constable's head, of a glistening white caravan, perhaps proudly flying the Constabulary's blue flag, was sufficient to carry the day and a modest budget had been allocated.

The resulting vehicle became known by those who had ever towed it, as the mobile brick. Constructed on a large caravan chassis, it had vertical sides, a flat roof, some windows and a door on the nearside. The headroom inside was generous. A tiny compartment at the front contained a chemical toilet. A modest cupboard housed a two-burner Calor gas stove and a small sink with a rudimentary water supply and waste tank. Across the centre was a waist high counter top with a lifting flap. A stack of a dozen folding chairs were held firmly in place with a fabric strap. Over the drawbar a box contained two gas cylinders. There were batteries and a cable link to a towing vehicle's charging system to provide lighting. Even though seldom used, like all police vehicles, the MPS was kept fully maintained, ready for action.

All police officers are trained to varying standards to drive panda cars, area cars, CID cars, dog vans and the like. At some point in their careers, some follow a popular ambition to become traffic officers, involving high speed pursuits and so on. They are given the highest of advanced training, including familiarity with all kinds of vehicles, from tractors to heavy goods vehicles and buses. And how to tow caravans and trailers.

Such an officer is PC George Lusty. Fresh in his mind this morning were the long hours he had spent on the icy, accident littered roads of yesterday. Today he reported for duty at 0545 in readiness for his morning shift. At least it was a bit warmer today.

"Good morning Sarge," he greeted the Traffic Sergeant, who said, "I've got a nice little job for you this lovely Saturday morning, Lusty. Take the Land Rover and the MPS."

He handed PC Lusty a message sheet which briefly said, 'Saturday 8th November. Take mobile police station to be parked at end of Beech Street, Millwood, near iron railings, by 0800 hours. Hand over to West Division CID. Leave parked there and return to Traffic Division'.

PC Lusty had never towed the mobile brick before but he knew of its reputation for having a tail which wagged the dog. He'd have to take it slowly. It is some twenty miles to Millwood. He'd better get cracking. He was an officer who didn't rely on the canteen but preferred to bring a flask and sandwiches. He would get his breakfast once he'd come clear at Millwood.

◆ ◆ ◆

DC Richard Harlow sat in the pool car, parked and waiting in Beech Street. He was idly reflecting on CID pool cars. This one was very anonymous, a three year old beige Austin Allegro. He knew the police workshops maintained and tuned even CID pool cars to a high standard. He smiled to himself as he had on at least one occasion surprised some fleeing criminals, just using the agility of such a car. He glanced occasionally in the mirror. At 0749 he saw the Traffic Division Land Rover, towing the mobile police station, turning sedately into the street and then gingerly squeezing between a few cars parked almost opposite each other. The driver parked the Land Rover by the iron gate with the MPS neatly aligned behind it.

"Impressive bit of parking," he said to PC Lusty as they greeted one another.

PC Lusty grinned, "It's that murder is it? Heard a bit on the radio yesterday about a body found in a wood. Is this the wood? How's it going?"

DC Harlow nodded and patted the side of the MPS, "Early days yet. I think the DI hopes this thing will attract the locals to come forward with information. The local Nick's some distance away. I'm only here till 1200. I've got to go to the PM with the boss this afternoon." That thought hadn't really left DC Harlow's mind since the night before.

"Rather you than me. So much for CID, eh?" said Lusty.

Just then, PC Stevens walked down the street.

"I've been sent along to keep you company this morning," he said, "I'm often on this beat. People know me and might open up."

PC Lusty was winding down the steadies at each corner of the caravan chassis when a loud shout came from across the street.

"Oi! You! Ye'r not leavin' that ruddy thing there are yer?" the voice wanted to know. It was the older Mr. Tallow, standing at his front door with unkempt hair and dressed in what appeared to be a vest and pyjama trousers.

PC Lusty turned and called back, "Good morning, Sir. It's the mobile police station to do with the incident in the woods. It won't be here more than a couple of days."

"A couple er days? 'Ow d'yer reckon I'm gonna get me lorry in an' out er these gates with that bleedin' thing parked across 'em?" said Tallow. "Shift it!" he commanded.

Realisation dawned on PC Lusty. He should have spotted that. Appeasement was needed. "Sorry, Sir. I should have thought you might have a lorry. No worries. I'll shift it back a bit."

Tallow disappeared. The MPS was carefully reversed a length backwards. It was still alongside the iron railings but now well clear of the brown gates opposite. Lusty finished setting it up and disconnected it from the Land Rover. He turned that around and, with a raised hand and a wide grin, was gone. He was thinking of the first layby on the main road out of Millwood, his flask of coffee and his sandwiches.

DC Harlow stepped inside the MPS and quickly discovered several things. Firstly there was no heating. The focus for this vehicle had been shows and gymkhanas on warm summer days. Happily, today was a few degrees warmer than yesterday. He had anticipated there might be a gas stove (and the kettle in the cupboard below) and had brought some tea making supplies. Opening the cupboard under the central counter he found two notice boards faced with white plastic and a box of coloured marker pens. On a shelf there was a supply of official forms, statement forms, message pads and so on.

"Shall we get a few chairs set out?" he suggested to PC Stevens, "You never know how busy it might get. I'll do a couple of notices." On the boards he wrote in large letters, 'MURDER. Thursday Evening. Do you have information? Please call in here or contact your local Police Station'. He placed one of these leaning against the rear end of the MPS, facing up the street. The other he placed next to the open door. "That should do for now," he said, then turned to the kettle.

◆ ◆ ◆

At about the same time, DI Merton was at his desk and opening two large brown envelopes. One contained a substantial set of large, glossy colour photographs recording the scene in the woods and the body, all in clear crisp detail. The other contained preliminary forensics reports. He glanced through them, not noticing much that he didn't already suspect. He put the envelope with the photographs on the table near the pin board. Taylor could now make use of them. He put the reports in his old briefcase, grabbed his coat and went downstairs. To the desk sergeant he said, "As you can guess, we're going to be busy for a bit. If anything comes in for us, either get uniform to do it or pass it upstairs."

He drove to Millwood.

♦ ♦ ♦

DI Merton used the flat of his hand to bang loudly on the main front door of the *George and Dragon* and shouted, "Police." During much of the morning, the landlord, Geoffrey, was busy in the bar clearing up from last night and preparing for the day ahead. He opened the door, looked at Merton and said, "You were in yesterday." Merton agreed, showed his warrant card and said, "A few words if you don't mind."

Geoffrey ushered him in, re-bolting the door.

"Sad business. All we've heard is a body's been found in the woods behind us. Was it a tramp or maybe somebody overdosed on drugs or something? People say there's hippies in the woods taking drugs, and that."

Geoffrey was clearly a busy young man, his sleeves rolled up and with a cloth in his hand. Merton said, "Can we sit down for a few minutes please? I'd like your help if you wouldn't mind."

"I've got to get this finished. Busiest day, Saturday. Open at 12. Cellar to do." Geoffrey was usually a calm individual but he now seemed a bit flustered.

"I'll be as quick as I can. Do you know anything about what happened?" said Merton, trying to work out why the man seemed to be a bit bothered. He could certainly talk.

"No. Everybody's been talking about it in the pub. The news didn't say much about it yesterday. They keep going on about a body in the woods. Sounds a bit odd. A bit like Agatha Christie or something. They don't seem to know who it was. Who was killed, I mean."

DI Merton decided that, now the family had been informed, he needed Geoffrey's co-operation to enable the investigation to proceed. He said, "You have a darts team play here on a Thursday, don't you?"

Geoffrey nodded. "I've only been here a couple of years but I think they've been going for just about ever. Not the darts team, the club. A sort of club. Well, ever since they started just after the War. Yes, as long ago as that. Started by some RAF types from the base but I don't think there's many of those now. One's got one of those handlebar moustaches the RAF types wear. I don't think he was a pilot though. Rob, that's it. Call themselves the Thursday Club. Nice bunch. Good business. They're in a league. Sometimes play away but they were here on Thursday. Practising for a big match, I think. That's one of the shields they won, on the wall," concluded Geoffrey, pointing.

Merton patiently let him finish. "Are there any women in this, er, Thursday Club?"

"It's mostly men. Getting on a bit most of them. But, yes, there's Janet. She's Raymond's wife I think. But Sally's the sweetheart. All the men love Sally. She's quite a bit younger and a bit of a stunner. For her age, I mean. She's on her own I think. There's no hanky-panky goes on though. Don't think so anyway. They're all just good company with each other. Goodness knows how Sally became part of the darts team. Before my time. But she's good at darts."

"Thank you, Geoffrey. You're being a big help," said Merton. Geoffrey relaxed a little. Merton looked him straight in the eye. "I now need to tell you something because I need you to help me. I need you to give me a list, as much as you can, of all the members of this Thursday Club, because it was one of their members who died on Thursday evening. It was Sally Weston."

Geoffrey went suddenly quiet. Eventually he asked, "No, can't be ... Sally? ... no ... oh no ... lovely Sally ... can't be ... What happened?"

"That's what we have to find out. The list of members will help. How many are there? Do any of them come in at any time besides Thursdays?"

Geoffrey collected himself enough to be able to start remembering. "Not sure I know all their names. Bit of a blur really. There's Fred. I know him because he always seems to be first in and we sometimes have a chat. Ray - that's Raymond - and Janet, like I said. There's Jim. Rob - I told you he has a handlebar moustache. There's one called Dylan. Sounds Welsh doesn't it, like Dylan Thomas. There's Bruce ... he's RAF as well, I think ... and Tom. Tom was late in on Thursday. Missed the darts. Only had a half. Can't think of the others. Oh, silly me, there's Jim of course."

There was a pause and Geoffrey's head sank, "Oh, no, no .. poor Sally. Who could have ...?" He pulled himself together, "What happened to her?"

Merton had been writing the names in his notebook. He repeated that the police were trying to find out what had happened. He asked, "Do you know where any of these people live. We'll need to speak to them all as soon as possible. Before next Thursday."

"No, I haven't a clue really. Mostly local I guess. One or two come by car. I sometimes see them coming in from the car park. Hang on, we call on Fred sometimes. He set himself up as a bit of a handyman when he retired. He's done the odd job for us now and then. Might have his card." He rummaged in a draw under the till behind the bar. "Yes, here it is."

Merton wrote an address and telephone number in his notebook. He said, "Just one more thing. Do you know what time Sally left here on Thursday. Did she go with anyone?"

"They just gradually go in dribs and drabs usually. At a guess between 9.30 and 10. I didn't notice particularly."

"Do you mind if I use your gents?" Merton asked.

"It's through there."

When Merton returned, Geoffrey was looking at a large black diary, "I've just remembered. When he was here on Thursday, Ray booked a table for two for Sunday lunch. Tomorrow. For him and Janet I expect. One o'clock." We normally just do snacks and things, here in the bar. But on Sundays we set up a carvery in the lounge, through there. It's very popular."

"Thanks," said Merton. "Do you take a phone number with bookings?"

"We normally would but not always when we know them as regulars," said Geoffrey. "There's not one here. His name's Ray Lowesby."

"Do you have any tables left for lunch tomorrow? For two? Say one o'clock?" asked Merton.

"It's a bit late now," Geoffrey was studying the diary. "Sometimes we can squeeze an extra table in if really necessary. Yes we could do that. For two you say?"

He wrote DI Merton's booking in the diary.

"Thank you. You've been very helpful, Mr. er…?."

"Smith. Geoffrey Smith," he said.

"The radio and newspapers will have the information about it being Sally very soon, no doubt by this evening," said Merton. "In the meantime, if you should happen to see any of the people who knew Sally I should be careful what you say. Bound to be upsetting for some of them. I'll see you tomorrow then."

Geoffrey Smith nodded while he was pondering the reason why the detective wanted to come for lunch tomorrow. Right in the middle of a murder investigation. He let DI Merton through the door.

Outside, Merton strolled thoughtfully around the pub a couple of times. He wasn't in a hurry. Somehow, the whole case seemed to centre on this place. Standing in the road looking at the building he saw a traditional old black and white double-fronted public house with a central front door accessed up three steps. The sign of the *George and Dragon* was a large one, hanging over the door. To the right was the entrance to the car park. To the left began a row of small shops but there was the gap, about six feet wide, leading into a footpath, the one where the hapless PC had stood guard yesterday, next to the kitchen window.

He walked along the footpath with the pub on his right. There was the side door bearing a sign which said 'BAR'. The car park extended around the back of the building all the way to the footpath which was separated from it by a brown close boarded fence with a pedestrian gap in it. Merton strolled into the car park and noted another door into the building which would give more direct access to the car park. It also had a sign, 'LOUNGE & BAR'.

Returning to the footpath he walked slowly

along it. He guessed it was no more than 100 yards long, perhaps a bit less. There were two very old and very vandalised lamp posts which, one day long ago, might have given out a dim light. The brown fence on the right enclosing the car park continued all the way to join the now familiar grey fence with the gap in it. Once, before the fence had been replaced, there had been a proper gate into the wood. The footpath turned left at the end, giving access through a series of gates to the rear yards of the shop premises.

DI Merton looked more closely at the gap in the fence than he had done yesterday. He guessed that vandals had created it as a shortcut. The debris was still lying around on the woodland side. The timber had no doubt been treated and so hadn't rotted. It was clear that the murder weapon had once been a piece of the middle rail. The top and bottom rails were still intact. He stooped and squeezed through the gap and stood for a few minutes, staring at the spot where Sally's body had been found. There was now nothing to see unless you looked closely for some blood on the brambles.

He turned, stared for a long time at the gap in the fence and speculated about the possibilities. He still could not see anyone waiting for Sally to use this as a shortcut to get home. It wasn't really on, was it? Or would she? He couldn't make up his mind. No good guessing. But then … no, the killer must be known to her, surely? They must have had a reason to come to this spot together. He tried hard to think of one. Was it someone from the pub? The Thursday Club? Or someone else altogether who she had arranged to meet. Surely nobody would have wanted to hang about on such a freezing night. A thought occurred to him. The drugs business that Harris and Taylor were looking into. That was around here somewhere. Was Sally into that scene? Surely not. Far too cold for anybody.

DI Merton decided this was not going to be an open and shut case, as he had first thought it might be. Far from it. He strode back along the footpath to retrieve his car and drove around to Beech Street.

❖ ❖ ❖

DS Harris and Taylor had arranged to meet up at DHQ and drive in the other CID pool car to Beech Street. They looked in at the MPS, told DC Harlow they would be back by 1200, then walked the short distance to knock on Margaret's door. It was opened by a man in his fifties who looked dishevelled and as though he had the weight of the world on his shoulders. They introduced themselves. This was Graham, Sally and Margaret's older brother. Taylor told him that it was she who had been with Margaret yesterday.

"Thank you so much for all you did. It made a big difference," said Graham. "Come in," he said. Margaret made an effort to smile when she saw Taylor, who thought she probably hadn't slept very much again.

"This is my wife, Sarah," said Graham. 'she came with me. She's been a big help." Sarah didn't say very much but made teas and coffees for everyone while they spent a few minutes checking that Margaret was managing alright for the moment.

Sergeant Harris explained that this was just a brief visit to keep in touch. He asked if they would mind if he and Taylor had a look in Sally's bedroom because it sometimes helped with the investigation. Graham pointed the way up the dark stairs. From the landing they opened the door he had indicated and went in. It was a plain room with pale mauve wallpaper. The white furnishings were simple, appearing to be the self-assembly type made from compressed board. The exception was the wardrobe which was freestanding, wooden and quite large for the size of the room. A tall mirror had been fixed to one door.

After a few minutes, Taylor said, "She'd got some nice things. Clothes. And look at this jewellery box. It's got a lot of bits and bobs in it. Nothing valuable, but nice." There were a few pictures on the wall. A black and white photo of two young women and a young man. Taylor assumed it might be the two sisters and Sally's husband in happier times before the crash. She looked closely at Sally's left hand in the picture and could just tell there was a wedding ring and another ring visible. She had been certain there were no rings on her finger yesterday. A small colour photograph in a white frame showed a baby laying on the lap of a woman who was bending over so her face was not visible.

Downstairs, Harris said they were sure to need to come and talk to the family again and went to the front door. Graham followed to let them out.

DS Harris paused and said quietly to Graham, "Don't be alarmed. A few questions. It's just routine. We do it to everyone I'm afraid. What work do you do?"

Graham said, "I'm a tube train driver. Northern line."

"That's shift work presumably. What shifts have you been on the last few days?"

Graham did look slightly alarmed at the questioning but said, "It's varied a bit but it was basically mornings all last week. This weekend happens to be my weekend off and I'm supposed to be on lates this coming week but I'm hoping they'll give me compassionate leave." Tears welled into his eyes.

Harris said, "As I say, Sir, just routine, we ask everyone. Where were you on Thursday evening?"

"I was at home. Finchley," said Graham.

◆ ◆ ◆

By mid-morning, most townspeople knew about the body found in the woods yesterday. Radios were tuned to the hourly local radio bulletins. Some, from behind twitching curtains in Beech Street had seen the activity at number 66 yesterday and speculation was spreading.

At one point, Mrs. Robertson had come out to clean her front windows, for the second time that week. A few others were finding excuses to stand on the pavement chatting to one another, despite the chill.

Nobody, it became clear to DC Harlow and PC Stevens, had any information. Why would they, really? By eleven o'clock their tea kettle had boiled at least three times. Occasionally one or other of them slowly walked the length of the street, exchanging a few commiserations with those watching. Just after eleven, PC Stevens became aware of a small boy in the doorway. He was standing on the step to look inside.

"Hello, who are you?" said Stevens, thinking that the lad looked about nine years old.

"Pete," said Pete who looked cold, wearing just shirt, trousers and a sleeveless pullover.

"Do you want to come and see inside?"

"Yeah." Pete stepped no further than just inside the doorway and looked around, not seeing very much of interest. "What do you do in here?" he wanted to know.

"Well," said PC Stevens, treading cautiously, "If anybody wants to come and tell the police anything, they can come and tell us here." he said.

Pete said nothing for a little while. He was thinking. Both officers waited. Suddenly Pete said, "I seen them go into the wood the other night. There were four of them."

DC Harlow spoke gently, "Hello Pete. My name's Richard. Which night was that?"

"Not last night. The one before. It were the one with the big moon lighting up the place so I could see. Really bright it were," said Pete.

"Were you out in the street as well, then?" wondered Harlow.

"Me Dad don't come home from work till eight. He's on shifts at the concrete works. Me Mam was round at gran's in Sycamore Street.

She gets back to get me and me Dad's tea. Gran's poorly. Sometimes I come out on me bike but it were too cold then. But I were looking at the moon out me window. When me Dad got home I had to go down for me tea."

"These people you saw going into the wood. Do you know if they were men or women?"

"Dunno. They came down the street and went into the wood. All dressed in black. Dunno," he repeated, shrugging his shoulders.

"Was it long after that you had to go down for your tea?"

"No, 'bout five minutes."

"Where do you live, Pete?"

Pete pointed vaguely across the road. "59," he said.

"Listen Pete," said DC Harlow, "You've been really helpful. I'll write all that down and it could be very useful. Good lad."

Just then, there was a yell from outside. A woman's voice was shouting, "Pete, what you doing in there?" Pete turned and was gone.

DC Harlow smiled at PC Stevens and shrugged. "You never know." He wrote down everything Pete had told them onto a message pad.

After that, a handful of local people, one by one, put their heads through the open door asking if there was any news. Whatever was going through their minds was left unsaid.

❖ ❖ ❖

DS Harris and DC Taylor walked the short distance back from Margaret's house to the MPS and went inside. "Not very cosy in here, is it?" said Harris. It was about 11.45.

"Cup of tea, Sarge?" said Harlow.

He asked the same question of DI Merton when he eventually arrived just after midday.

"Thanks," he said. "We're alright for time, Harlow. Just a quick recap then. Taylor, you're here this afternoon?" "Yes, Sir," she said. Merton looked at PC Stevens who said, "My relief should be here any minute, Sir."

DS Harris related briefly what he and Taylor had been doing that morning. Merton said to him, "Stay here if you like but you'll be wanting to get back to your girl to talk about houses. You can get on back to her now if you like. Tomorrow, I want you to keep a general eye on this place, along with Harlow. Sort it out between you. There should be a PC here as well. Okay?"

"Thank you, that's great. Yes, Sir," said Harris.

"Come on then Harlow, Let's get this thing done." Harlow tossed the pool car keys to Taylor.

Just as they were stepping out of the door, Merton looked back, smiled at Taylor and said, "As for you, Taylor, it'll be your lucky day tomorrow. I'm taking you out on a lunch date. Meet me here at 1200 hours. Don't get too excited. We'll be on duty. Don't look like a detective."

◆ ◆ ◆

PC O'Brien arrived in a panda car a few minutes later to relieve PC Stevens.

"Busy?" he said to Taylor who was still pondering what Merton had said about a lunch date tomorrow. Curious. Where? When? Why? No doubt it would become clear. Anyway, somehow she hadn't been expecting to get this Sunday off.

"Oh, yes, hello," she said. "Actually no. I don't think it's been busy but I've only just got here myself."

It seemed that the one o'clock local news was now carrying the story in more detail. They were saying the name of the deceased had now been released as relatives had been informed. Sally Weston was being described by the media as 'the body in the wood'.

"You went with DS Harris yesterday to get a statement from the chap who called it in, didn't you? Morgan, I think," she said to O'Brien. He nodded.

"He was in a bit of a state wasn't he?" she asked.

"Well, I think by the time we got there he wasn't too bad. He'd obviously been well shaken up by what he'd seen, even though he must have seen bodies before. He's retired from the ambulance service. RAF during the war. His wife was nice, she was fussing around him. He'll be alright."

Beech Street was normally very quiet. Not many residents owned cars. Just then they heard a noisy vehicle approaching. Through the window they saw a small, almost vintage, green Bedford lorry approaching. It turned across in front of the MPS and reversed up to the brown gates opposite. Its horn sounded. Soon afterwards the gates opened and the lorry reversed into the yard beyond. They had a glimpse of the piles of scrap metal and, through a gap could make out two railway wagons beyond them. The gates closed and all was silent.

Taylor was thinking. She said, "if we see that lorry come out, I'd like its reg. number. I'm sure I've seen it before."

She sat quietly, looking out of the window at the brown gates. It dawned on her that the last time she had seen that lorry it had been parked in a side street next to the Second Chance shop which she and Harris had visited the other day. There had been no reason to take note of it before.

A few more minutes passed. She said, "Got it!"

"What's that?" said a surprised O'Brien.

"Look at that sign." Taylor was looking across the road at the 'Tallows Metal Dealers' sign. "It's exactly the same shade of yellow as the sign at the second-hand shop Harris and I went to the other day to recover some stolen silver. There's still a lot more to recover. I wonder …"

CHAPTER 10

The naked, blue-grey body of Sally Weston lay on a white ceramic slab, one of four in a row in the post mortem room. As it was a Saturday, the other slabs were not occupied. Dr. Franklyn and his assistant were carrying out the meticulous, required processes of a forensic post mortem.

DC Richard Harlow was standing close to Sally Weston's feet, next to DI Merton. He was trying not to look at her damaged body, preferring to concentrate on the odd fact that the row of slabs appeared, to him, rather like a row of sacrificial altars in some ancient temple. When Dr. Franklyn had approached Sally's chest with a large scalpel blade, Harlow had fleetingly considered turning and briskly leaving the room. The moment passed as he reluctantly decided the shame of it might be too much. He was determined not to make a spectacle of himself. He was surprised there was no blood.

But it really wasn't going well. He was aware of DI Merton occasionally speaking to Dr. Franklyn who sometimes replied. Harlow wasn't quite sure what they were saying. The persistent buzzing in his ears made their voices distorted. His vision was blurred and he felt light-headed and hot. Somehow he was looking down on the scene from a distance.

DC Harlow had never seen a naked female body before. He was 26 years old and had hopes that his current new girlfriend might prove to be the one he would propose to. There had been two or three girlfriends before. Somehow, life and interests and football and time at the pub with his mates had got in the way a bit. Mostly, the unsocial hours of his seven year police career hadn't helped. The joys of married life were still to come, he always hoped. Quite soon maybe.

Somehow, these thoughts had rushed through and taken charge of his head. Keeping his eyes averted had helped.

Some time passed. Harlow didn't know how long but his head seemed slightly clearer. He heard Franklyn say something about stomach contents … alcohol … looks like cherries … so just guessing … maybe Martinis … two or three maybe …lab will confirm next week … and no … no sex around the time of death … yes … before midnight … from around 9pm.

The continuous buzzing abruptly stopped. Harlow's head almost cleared as he recognised his name. "Detective Constable Harlow is it?" He forced his eyes to focus as he heard it spoken by Dr. Franklyn. "Still upright then? Not all of them manage that. Well done, lad."

"Thank you, Sir" he said. DI Merton was chuckling. Harlow still tried not to look at Sally but he found that now she was all sown up again it didn't matter quite so much and it wasn't really affecting him at all.

"Now then," Dr. Franklyn went on without pausing, "The weapon. Your lump of wood with blood on it. Lab's done their job. You should have the report. It's her blood alright so open and shut case. Well ... almost. Obviously no fingerprints. Here it is." He turned and picked up the timber from a side table, still wrapped in its plastic evidence bag. He removed it and placed the square bloody end against Sally's horribly smashed temple. "Perfect fit, you see?" he said triumphantly. "Must have been an almighty blow. Right-handed assailant - must be - but used both arms in a mighty swing, like this, I'm pretty sure." Franklyn demonstrated the swing, arms outstretched, holding the timber like a cricket bat going for a six.

"Got to have been a man to make such a mess of her skull. A strong man at that. Even without the dent the brain wouldn't have taken kindly to that force. Ruptured the artery, of course, so she lost a lot of her blood pretty quickly too. There's your causes of death. Take your pick. Unless the lab comes up with anything in the Martinis. That's unlikely. I can't find anything else."

"Thanks, Doc," said DI Merton. "Just a couple of things occur to me. Does she have any abrasions anywhere else? Has she been dragged?"

"Well, first have a look at this. You can see she has a good bruise on her left lower arm. In fact her ulna is fractured. Even that took a bit of force. My guess is she put her arm up to defend herself. Corresponding marks on her coat sleeve. That was really painful so she dropped her arm, then he took an even mightier swing at her head. The force somehow spun her round and she dropped on the spot. Doubt she was dragged. No particular marks on the boots. Clothes otherwise all pretty clean. Oh, a few scratches on the other side of her face but that was the brambles she fell into …"

"And I guess the other thing you want to know is … will there be any blood on the attacker?" Merton nodded. "Simple answer … I dunno … blood would certainly have spurted but if he was holding that long-ish bit of wood, arm outstretched in a swinging motion… Jacket sleeves maybe. Maybe too far away, maybe not."

The mortuary assistant covered Sally Weston's body with a sheet. The brown label attached to her big toe was still visible. She was transferred to a trolley, raised up and slid, head first, into a vacant fridge.

◆ ◆ ◆

As they left the building, DC Harlow found the fresh cool air very welcome. The car headed back towards Millwood. Neither man spoke for a while. DC Harlow was deep in thought, reflecting on his vivid experience. Before entering that post mortem room he had felt, perhaps, a little gung-ho about the whole thing. He had even wondered, briefly, if the experience might be a bit sexy. That thought had quickly been wiped from his mind. It had been nothing of the kind. Nowhere near. Through the haze of his first really close-up encounter with death, he had become aware that he was looking at a human being who, less than two days ago, had been full of life, laughing, playing darts in the company of friends, drinking Martinis. Sally would never do that again. The life of her sister Margaret had been devastatingly changed, too.

The experience had saddened and made a deep impression on DC Harlow. He would never forget it. One day he would think back and describe it to himself as almost a spiritual experience, one which made him a more compassionate, a more conscientious and determined police officer.

On the journey back, to deflect his mind from those thoughts, he told DI Merton the slightly odd tale which the young lad, Pete, had related.

"What? In that cold? It was bitter. Surely not. The drugs connection presumably. If not, what else?" Merton was trying hard but failing to think of any connection to the murder. He was still thinking that surely there's no way a woman like Sally would enjoy an evening with friends playing darts and then go into a really cold, dark wood to take drugs. It just doesn't fit. He'd already decided there was no way that she would use the wood as a shortcut, only to be pounced on and killed by some spaced out hippies. She still had her handbag for one thing.

DC Harlow was refreshing his mind and thinking aloud, "Full moon, drugs, midnight rituals, howling wolves ...."

DI Merton was speculating, "Is the lad certain it was Thursday night? Yes, it was a big full moon. I'd nipped out to the chip shop for my supper and saw it. But the moon is still big for a couple of days either side of full moon. Was it cloudy on Wednesday? Or Tuesday? Can't remember. When we get to the office on Monday, Harlow, check that. Some meteorological place somewhere will know if there were clouds over Millwood. But if the lad's right, perhaps we ought to check it out. When we get a minute."

"Right. Now, to today. One more job to do. I've got the address of just one member of this Thursday Club so far. It's a Fred, er, Mellor. We'll call on him."

The Rover parked outside an unassuming house hiding behind a tall privet hedge in Dover Avenue, not far from Millwood town centre. The door was answered by an older man with grey hair who looked inquiringly at them.

"It's the police, Sir," showing warrant cards. "DI Millwood and DC Harlow. Sorry to disturb you. Is it Mr. Mellor?"

"Yes. I suppose it's about Sally. Terrible. Terrible. Couldn't believe it. Only with her on Thursday. At the *George*. Darts."

"May we come in, Mr. Mellor? It's just a few inquiries. We need to speak to people who knew Sally."

"Yes, of course. I should think everybody is in shock. What on earth could have happened?"

"That's what we need to find out. I believe you were at the *George and Dragon* on Thursday evening? When did you get there and when did you leave?"

"I'm often the first there. About quarter to seven. I usually get some drinks in. We had a friendly match. Practice for next week's league match. Oh, no. Next week. Maybe we won't do that next week. It might be called off in the .... Respect for Sally ... Yes, sorry, most of us leave around 9.30. Especially these dark evenings. Then it's a short walk back here for me."

"Did you see Sally leave?"

"No. I'm first in, first out usually. That's me. I'm sure she was still there when I went. There's always someone still chatting to Sally. For an old fogey like me, I like to get home to see Anna Ford on News at Ten."

"Do you know where Sally lived?"

"Well ... now you mention it ... no I don't. Can't have been far though. She didn't come by car or anything. Didn't really know that much about her, come to think of it. But she was good company. Good at darts, too."

Fred's wife came into the room. He told her that these gentlemen were from the police and were asking about Sally.

"I think the men will all miss her," she said, looking knowingly at her husband.

"Did you know her, Mrs. Mellor?" DI Merton asked.

"Not very well, no. We did sometimes meet up when there was a bit of a party or something arranged. Some wives went to them, like at Christmas. There's been one or two summer outings as well, over the years. I don't think Sally ever went on any of those. Probably got commitments at home at weekends. Wouldn't be surprised. Yes, Sally was nice but she's not ... she wasn't one to stand any nonsense. She knew her mind, as far as I could tell," Mrs Mellor concluded.

"So, Mr. Mellor, you have no knowledge of Sally, her circumstances, or have had any involvement with her other than on Thursday evenings at the Thursday Club?"

"No, none at all," said Fred Mellor.

"Finally, I'd like to ask for your help please. We still need to speak to the other members. Can you help us with the addresses of any of them? Or telephone numbers?" said DI Merton.

Fred thought for a moment, "Funny thing, all these years, you'd think I'd know where they lived, wouldn't you? Well, I know Tom and Jim are just up the street from here. Jim's just around the corner at the top ... the posh houses in Brighton Crescent. Not sure of house numbers. Oh, Bruce is in Lyndon Avenue. That's in that direction. The other side of Main Street. I gave him a hand building a new garden shed. He couldn't really manage it himself. That was in the summer. His wife's the gardener. I do a few odd jobs for people. They're the ones that live this end of town anyway. The others'll be in the book. Oh, yes, Norman's in Station Road, just across from the *George*."

DC Harlow was making notes.

"Thank you both," said DI Merton. "If we need a statement or have any other questions, we'll see you again."

Back in the car Merton said, "No more now. It's about dark." They returned to the office. "Good show today. See you tomorrow."

"Yes. Thank you, Sir. Goodnight," replied DC Harlow.

❖ ❖ ❖

By 1600 hours a few more people had called in at the MPS, mainly to satisfy their curiosity, some to ask how they could express their condolences. None had any information which might be helpful.

The old Bedford lorry had reappeared through the brown gates and driven off. It's registration number had been noted.

In the gathering gloom and chill, Taylor and PC O'Brien agreed enough was enough.

PC O'Brien said that he would keep an eye on

the MPS for the rest of his duty and would get the overnight panda crew to do the same. He said, If you let me have the keys I'll get the morning beat man to bring them around at 0800.

They locked the door and left the Chief Constable's pride and joy to its own devices overnight in Beech Street, opposite the scrap yard.

Taylor drove the CID pool car back to DHQ, making a short diversion to pass the 'Second Chance' shop and to note that the small, green lorry was parked just inside the side street.

CHAPTER 11

Detective Sergeant Dave Harris had welcomed the unexpected half day off he had been given yesterday. It could so easily have been him joining the DI at the post mortem. He had been to a few and never really relished the prospect. Harlow needed that initiation. The afternoon relaxing with Susan had been enjoyable and had helped to sort out his head. This morning, a Sunday after all, and given his fairly loose instructions, or maybe simply because it was a Sunday, he decided to have a lie in. Of course, within minutes, he was feeling guilty and so was out of his flat almost as early as usual. He got to the MPS just after nine and had a chat over a brew with the lads.

"This thing's going back tonight. I'm not really sure how useful it's been," said Harris.

All was quiet until Graham Finlay called in around mid-morning to ask if there was any news. He and Margaret and Sarah were finding the waiting difficult and felt the need to know what was happening. DS Harris told him that the CID team were pursuing inquiries and more would be happening tomorrow and during the week ahead. He said it was quite likely the Inspector would want to talk to them some more. He made tentative arrangements to call in tomorrow. Graham Finlay seemed pleased with that and left.

About half an hour later, a car arrived and parked nearby. The man who got out and came into the MPS was quite elderly but sprightly, well dressed and sporting a fine handlebar moustache.

"Can I ask someone about, about the, er, well I knew, er, Sally at the darts at the *George and Dragon*. It was on Thursday. It was in the paper this morning. Awful. Can't believe it. They said you were here ... had to come and find out."

"You'd better come in and have a sit down," said DS Harris. "Were you there on Thursday evening, Mr. ....?"

"Jordon, Rob Jordan. Robert, that is. Yes, it was Thursday. We had a friendly match. Sally ... good player. Good company ... nice ..." Rob Jordan was clearly upset.

"Can you tell me what you know about Sally."

"Only knew her at the Club. Not much else. I think she lived around here somewhere. Not sure. She was still there when I left on Thursday. Oh … no … it's so terrible. What happened to her?"

"We're working hard to find out, Mr. Jordan. That's why we're here."

"Was she in that wood when you found her then? How was … how was she killed. Do you know who did it?"

DS Harris said, "Mr. Jordan, these are all things we are looking into. It's too early to come to conclusions. I should wait at home. We are doing our best. Oh, what is your address, please, Sir?"

Jordon gave an address.

"Morton," said Harris, That's just on the far side of the RAF base, isn't it?"

"Yes, it's near the entrance to the base. I was serving there in the War. Same time as a few of the others. Adrian Cranmer lives near me. I usually give him a lift but he couldn't come last week. He was in Spain. He's still there."

DS Harris wrote down Adrian Cranmer's address," Thank you, Mr. Jordan. It's quite possible we will want to come and talk to you at home. We're talking to everyone who knew Sally. We will be in touch." Harris saw him to his car.

❖ ❖ ❖

Geoffrey Smith was dashing between kitchen, bar and lounge, with all the preparations necessary to run the *George and Dragon's* popular carvery on Sundays. He was glad only one party of early diners had arrived so far, to disturb his flow. Bar staff had arrived and were checking all was ready behind the bar, slicing lemons and that kind of thing.

Just after twelve, DI Merton came through the front door, noticing Geoffrey's hurried activity. "Don't worry, we're not here yet. Just want to check where our table is."

Without pausing, Geoffrey said, "Hello, it's you. Reserved labels on all the tables. Names on them." He disappeared into the kitchen.

Merton went through into the lounge. The carvery had been set up at the far end, in the alcove. Only one table was already occupied with four early diners. He glanced at the first table on the left, seemingly squeezed in just inside the door. There was a folded card which said 'Reserved. Merton'. He glanced at a few more tables, coming to one which was set for two. 'Reserved. Lowesby', it said. It was four tables away from his.

"Perfect," thought Merton. That had taken just a few minutes. He left and drove around to Beech Street, parking behind the MPS.

DC Harlow and DC Taylor were there and a constable he had not met before. The three were having a bit of a laugh about what the best dressed undercover detective should be wearing these days. Taylor had done her best to not look like a detective and more like a Sunday lunch date. She hoped her pale pink, floral patterned dress and complimentary darker reddish jacket would meet with approval.

DI Merton stepped inside and his glance at Taylor indicated that he did approve. "Sorry I'm a bit late. Checking up on something. We're in good time. Anything to report here?"

DC Harlow told him that it was still fairly quiet. He also said DS Harris had been there earlier and a couple of people had called in. One had been Graham Finlay, Sally's brother. "Sergeant Harris told him someone would call on him tomorrow morning, Sir." He checked his notes. "The other man was a Mr. Robert Jordan. He said he knew Sally from the Thursday Club and I think he wanted to find out what was happening. He seemed a bit jumpy. Sergeant Harris and Mr Jordan sat in that corner and had quite a chat. He's not long been gone but he said he'd be back here later this afternoon. DS Harris, that is, Sir."

DI Merton thought for a moment and said, "Good, thanks, Harlow. Right, Taylor, it's time for our date."

On the way back to the *George and Dragon* in the Rover he explained, "Taylor, this is all about trying to get a feel for the place - the pub. Then we might understand a bit more about this Thursday Club. We can't just wait until Thursday. Anyway, they might give their meeting a miss this week out of respect. I'm certain all this business - Sally, I mean - must be rooted in the place or in the club somehow. I don't buy this hippie, drugs, full moon thing. We'll have to check, of course. As to what we're doing now, if I were to go in for my lunch now, on my own, I'd stick out like the proverbial, wouldn't I? Better to be on a date with... who do you think ... my daughter, perhaps. Nice and casual. Oh, yes. For this, I'm John and you're Carol.

By this time they had arrived in the pub car park which was now quite full. Merton parked the car.

"Now then, we've got a table next to the door of the lounge. The landlord's told me that Raymond - Ray - Lowesby and his wife Janet are in for lunch at one o'clock, same as us. They've got a table four away from ours. They've probably got no more to do with it than any of the others. All I want to do is just see how they behave. It's an old idea from way back and sometimes you can pick something up. You keep an eye on Janet. When they, and we, are done eating, I might decide to have a word with them as they're leaving.

Taylor was taking all this in.

"By the way, we're on expenses. No fillet steak and maybe no pud. Depends on timing." They laughed, left the car and walked into the pub. Merton took Taylor's hand, holding it for effect as they went in. John Merton wished he was twenty years younger.

◆ ◆ ◆

"Well, we've got to eat, haven't we?" DI Merton responded to what was really an implied question from Taylor. She was still a bit uncertain of the reasoning behind their apparent extravagance while on duty.

The lunch date was going well. The two detectives were seated in such a way that they could casually glance down the room without drawing attention to what they were doing. They were tucking into their carvery meals - beef in Merton's case, with an extra Yorkshire pudding. Taylor had asked for a selection.

Keeping his voice low, he explained, between mouthfuls, "Carol, this might lead nowhere. We will simply interview all the members of this

Thursday Club, one by one. What will happen is that every one of them will say much the same thing, won't they? "We left the *George and Dragon* at about 9.30, give or take, can't quite remember and I or we walked or drove home, whichever was the case. Do you see that?"

Carol Taylor nodded in agreement.

Merton went on, "So, we need to try and separate them. Dig a bit deeper into the detail of what each one actually did. And of course to find out if any of them had any other connection with Sally, apart from this Thursday Club thing. The only exception, I think, was Norman. Don't know his other name. Apparently Norman stayed behind after the others had gone. Got another pint. That raises a question, doesn't it? Even though Sally had left earlier. Did Norman slip out to the gents, maybe? How long was he gone? We need those sort of details."

Taylor nodded again.

"But today we come to this couple here. Raymond and Janet Lowesby. I think they might be more interesting. It's is a long shot, I admit. Not so much because they might be suspects. I doubt that. The main reason is that they went out of the other door to the car park to drive home. It might depend where their car was parked but did they see anything? The fence between the footpath and the car park is around shoulder height.

Either they saw nothing - that's most likely I should think. Or they maybe saw Sally and someone else either with her or following her. That would be interesting, wouldn't it? It was dark of course, as well as being very cold, but the pub does have lights illuminating some of the car park."

Taylor agreed that would be very interesting.

"So," Merton took a couple of mouthfuls, paused and went on, "It goes back a few years but there was a study by a criminologist, what's his name, it'll come to me. I read it while I was prepping for my sergeants' exams I seem to remember. Basically it says that if you get an opportunity to study potential witnesses soon after an event, without them knowing, you might get a clue about whether they are purely innocent or maybe harbouring a guilty secret. So, if our couple down there appear to be having a perfectly normal happy husband and wife Sunday lunch that's one thing but if they are not acting as we would expect, that might be useful to know. Yes, it's a remote chance but when the landlord, Geoffrey, told me they'd booked a table I didn't want to pass it up. As I said, we've got to eat."

"Did you say you wanted to talk to them as well?" asked Taylor.

"It's not ideal, I know, accosting them just

after they've enjoyed their Sunday lunch out," Merton replied, "but these Thursday clubbers only seem to have vague ideas about where most of the others live. Can't quite understand that. So far we don't know where these two live so it's an opportunity to find out, as well as ask the usual questions. And I think they are the only couple in the Thursday Club so that makes them seem unlikely. But we've got to be careful before we eliminate anyone."

"Anyway, what do you think from what you've seen so far, Carol?"

Carol Taylor glanced along the room again. "They seem to be talking a lot to one another. Some couples do, don't they? Quite a lot hardly say anything to each other though?" She smiled. "Apart from that it all looks quite normal."

"Yes. This is likely to be a wild goose chase but I've enjoyed my lunch." They both laughed in agreement. Merton went on, "They don't seem quite done with their first course yet. We've done. Do you want a pud?"

Desserts were laid out on a separate table near the carvery. It was a self-service affair unless, a notice said, a warm steamed pudding with cream, ice cream or custard was required. Merton was tempted by a spotted dick and custard but decided it might take too long so they each selected a rum baba, which didn't take long to eat.

DI Merton had pre-paid for the two course meals on arrival and got the necessary receipt. He and Taylor left the lounge and stood in the wide hallway which connected the front and back doors of the pub and separated the lounge and bar. Several faded historical paintings depicting the history of the place were hung on the walls and they spent the next five minutes or so pretending to intently study them.

When the couple came through the door from the lounge, DI Merton approached them and said, "Mr. and Mrs. Lowesby? I really apologise for accosting you in this way but I wonder if you could spare us a few minutes."

The Lowesbys were surprised and Merton went on, "I am Detective Inspector Merton and this is my colleague, Detective Constable Taylor." They ensured that their identity cards could easily be seen and examined.

Merton went on, "Our problem is that we don't have an address for all of the members of the Thursday Club and we thought that perhaps you could help us please."

Mention of the Thursday Club was sufficient explanation and Raymond Lowesby said, "It's Sally, isn't it?"

"We could have a chat now or we could arrange to visit you at home if you would prefer, Sir," DI Merton said.

"No, we could do that here. Is that alright with you, dear? Mind you, it's shaken us up a lot. We were in two minds whether or not we wanted to come here today, weren't we dear? But I'd already booked the table when I was here on Thursday. So we thought a bit of normality would be a good thing and so we came."

"Thank you." Merton said. "Let's see if there's a quiet table in the bar. Perhaps a coffee? Unless you were going to have something else? Coffee alright for you, Taylor?"

Everyone agreed, a quiet table away from the bar was found and coffees ordered.

Raymond Lowesby smiled and asked the obvious question, "What are two police officers doing having Sunday pub lunches while they are on duty?" Clearly he had noticed them, only four tables away.

"Well, Sir. You'll appreciate that we are in the early stages of the investigation and this place is convenient. At the moment it is central to our inquiries. You'll no doubt also appreciate that even police officers have to eat."

Janet Lowesby, who so far hadn't spoken said, "Do you know what happened to poor Sally?"

DI Merton felt he had done too much talking. He picked up his coffee cup and glanced at Taylor, who understood and took the initiative.

DC Taylor said, "We are still trying to work that out. We know there are around ten members of the Thursday Club - a darts team. That's right, isn't it? We're obviously wanting to talk to everyone who knew Sally. We appreciate that Sally was a well-loved member who was good at darts. We must find out what happened to her. She left here about 9.30 on Thursday night, we believe?"

At that moment Raymond Lowesby abruptly stood up and took a few steps towards a tall man approaching them, carrying a half full beer glass. "Norman!" he greeted the man, "Didn't see you over there. How are you old man?"

"Spotted you from the other end of the bar. I see you're with friends. Won't keep you. Just thought I'd say hello." said Norman.

"No, no," Raymond said, "Not friends exactly. They're police. Talking to us about Sally. Have they talked to you?"

Norman's face dropped. "Do they know anything? When I heard ... awful ..." He went silent but came over to the table.

"Let's grab a chair for you," said Raymond, feeling better with greater numbers on his side. "This is Norman, Thursday Club. Knew Sally.

We're all pretty shook up by it all. Must be." Turning to Taylor he said, "Sorry, you were saying ..."

Merton interrupted, "I'm DI Merton and this is DC Taylor." They showed their warrant cards to Norman. "Is it alright, everyone, if we do this together, with Mr. er ... your name please?"

"Norman Wilson. It's alright with me," he said, accepting the situation. He continued, "I often call in here. My place is only five minutes away up Station Road. Where I live, that is. On my own. Convenient. They do amazing ham salad rolls. And ploughman's lunches. Oh, sorry, I'm rambling."

Raymond and Janet had nodded their agreement to a collective discussion.

"As I said," DC Taylor continued, "We're making inquiries and talking to everyone who knew Sally so that we can find out what happened to her. You were here on Thursday were you, Mr. Wilson?"

"What happened to her?" Norman had been taken aback slightly and had just realised the enormity of what they were talking about. "How ... I mean ... what happened to her ... where ...?"

DI Merton stepped in. "We're determined to find all that out. Now, Mr. Wilson, just to recap ... you're a member of the Thursday Club, I believe. You played darts on Thursday?" Norman was nodding. "What time did you leave?"

"I'm nearly always the last to go. Most of them seem to leave around half past nine, maybe a quarter to ten. Must be getting old, mustn't we? I usually have another pint. Hang around a bit. Nice, sitting by the fire. Have been known to doze off. No. Thursday? Must have been around ten. Yes, only saw part of the news when I got in. That's it. Left here about ten."

"Yes," Raymond chipped in, "Most of us do go around then. Half past nine, I mean. Some a bit later I suppose. We have a drive to do so we're usually gone around then." Janet was nodding in agreement.

"Whereabouts in the car park was your car parked on Thursday night, Mr. Lowesby?" DI Merton asked.

Raymond stiffened. "My car? Our car? Why? Oh, er, well I think on Thursday ... it wasn't very busy ... we parked near the back door ... you know ... just there." He pointed. He looked at Janet who nodded in agreement.

"When you went out to your car, can you remember seeing anyone? Either in the car park or maybe on the footpath just over the fence?"

The Lowesbys looked at one another. "No, don't think so. No. There was nobody about at all. I'm sure. We just got in the car and went home".

After a moment, Janet said, "Well, there was Rob. He usually goes at about the same time as us. We went out to the car park more or less together. No, on Thursday he came out a few minutes after us." Raymond agreed.

"And where is home, please?" asked Merton, writing down the address of the Lowesbys at Darrowton which he knew was a village about 20 minutes drive away.

"Thank you. And yours, Sir?"

"Just across the road from here. Station Road, Number 51." said Norman.

"That's been a very useful half an hour," said DI Merton. "Thank you for your time. We may need to speak to you again."

With that, Merton and Taylor left the *George and Dragon*.

"Blast it," said Merton, I forgot to get a receipt for those coffees!"

◆ ◆ ◆

"Did you have a good lunch, Sir?" DS Harris was grinning at Merton and Taylor as they arrived back at the MPS at about 1530 hours.

They agreed that the lunch and most importantly, they emphasised, the work they had done observing and interviewing no less than three

Thursday Club members, had been both enjoyable and useful.

DI Merton looked at Harris, DC Harlow and the constable and said, "I don't suppose you three have cracked the case this afternoon, either, have you?"

"Not quite, Sir." DC Harris's tongue was firmly in his cheek.

"Right then," said DI Merton. "I've told Traffic they can have this thing back at 1600 so they should be here very soon. I suppose it's been a bit of use, for reassurance if nothing else. We'll take the evening off and be back in the office at 0800 for a briefing to see where we are and what we do next. I've had a message that we'll have an extra couple of DCs from Central Division to lend a hand but as long as they get up to speed on what's going on I think we'll get them to catch up on some routine stuff. Can you sort them out on that DC Harlow? Give them a map, that sort of thing."

"And thanks, constable. You've had a fairly boring time of it."

"Not at all, Sir. It's been interesting. Learning a bit about CID and all that, Sir".

At 1600 hours the Traffic Division Land Rover drove down Beech Street and towed the MPS away.

CHAPTER 12

Six detectives sat around the desks in the CID office at West Division HQ, mugs of tea or coffee to hand. It was 0800 hours on Monday.

DI Merton stood and went over to the pin board where Taylor had pinned a street plan of the Millwood town area. He picked up three blank A4 sheets of paper and pinned them one above the other down the left side of the board. He selected a larger pin with a red top and carefully positioned it on the map, in the wood at the place where Sally's body had been found.

He said, "First, welcome to DC Firth and DC Oldroyd. They're here from Central Division to lend a hand. It's mainly so we can keep on top of the bread and butter stuff at the same time as we're doing this." He pointed to the red pin in the map. "I hope we don't keep you here for too long. We want to crack this as soon as we can, otherwise the Super won't be pleased. But for now, stay with us while we take a look at where we're at. You never know, any one of us could come up with something useful. All part of the team, aren't we?"

There was general agreement and a welcome for the two DCs.

DI Merton pointed at the pin board. "So, what have we really got so far? We've got a body and, frankly, a blank sheet of paper. Yes, we've spoken to a few people and broadly speaking everybody loved Sally. The Thursday Club members - those we've spoken to anyway - all left the *George and Dragon* and went home like good little children. We've got a vague notion about some folk getting themselves high on acid in the woods - actually not that far away from where the murder took place. They may or may not have been a factor on that night. Potentially I suppose they could be witnesses. We've spoken to Sally's sister Margaret and her brother and sister-in-law. Also, there's the place she worked - Armstrong's. They need a visit."

"What else do we know? DC Harlow!"

DC Harlow spluttered as he was drinking tea. "Well, Sir, we know how Sally was killed. Assailant facing her. Big lump of wood swung at her head. Bashed the side of her face in. Instant. Got to be a strong man. Open and shut. Sir," He was paraphrasing Dr. Franklyn.

"There you have it," said Merton, "'Straight from the horse's mouth. DC Harlow quite enjoyed his first post mortem on Saturday."

"Now for the big question," he continued. "What is that?"

After a few moments DC Taylor, now dressed more formally as a detective, said, "Motive, Sir. As far as I can see we have no idea why Sally was killed or whether it was random, pre-meditated, or what."

"Absolutely right." said DI Merton. Those Thursday Club people we've spoken to so far. All we've found out is roughly what time they've left the pub and, as I say, they all loved Sally. Our focus now has got to be to dig deeper with each one to see if they have some more personal connection with Sally. I have to admit - and I've thought long and hard - I can't think of anything else it might be. They all seem to have been such a happy bunch together, playing darts for Pete's sake."

"Let's have a plan," he went on. "Taylor, if you write a list of Thursday clubbers on that blank sheet. Nice big black writing with spaces so we can insert any significant detail. None get crossed off until we're totally sure about them."

From their notebooks, the detectives called

out the several names they had determined were members of the Thursday Club. Taylor wrote the list using a thick marker pen.

FRED MELLOR

RAYMOND AND JANET LOWESBY

ROBERT JORDAN

DYLAN ?

BRUCE MORGAN

TOM ?

JIM ?

NORMAN WILSON

ADRIAN CRANMER

"I think there's at least four there who we haven't spoken to at all yet," said Sergeant Harris. "We don't even know the full names of Dylan, Tom and Jim. Adrian Cranmer wasn't there on Thursday. By all accounts, he's in Spain."

"Right, Harris and Harlow, you get on to tracking down every one of those Thursday Club members." said Merton. "The ones we've seen know we might want another word. But make sure you dig deep enough to find out if any of them had a deeper relationship with Sally than playing darts. Maybe some phone calls first, I suggest. It'll take a bit of co-ordinating. Maybe even a few days. We need a tick by every one of those names."

"Even Bruce Morgan, Sir?" asked Harris. "I took the routine statement from him about his finding the body. Do we need another interview with him?"

"Don't see why not," said Merton. "What do you think? If nothing else, he might know something about another Club member which might be useful. It's a good point though. Just shows how deep we need to go."

DI Merton then said, "Taylor and I are going to look at it from the other side of the coin. Sally's relatives. They're devastated so we've not pressed too hard so far. But by now they might be able to talk to us in a bit of depth about Sally's past. It's a bit of a mystery at the moment. Even the Club members we've already spoken to tell us they don't even know where she lived. We'll see about that. Taylor, will you phone them and see if they're okay for us to call in this morning for another chat. Don't tell them why. Just say we want to stay in touch."

Yes, Sir," said Taylor, moving to a desk in the corner with a phone.

"I want to fit in a visit to Armstrong's as well today if I can. Perhaps while we're around there."

"Excuse me, Sir." It was DC Oldroyd, the older of the two detectives from Central Division. "It may be of no value at all but I am one of the on-call Force Drug Squad team. We've not been going long and it's only small scale yet but the drug problem's growing. Anyway, I thought I might be able to help with these reports of drug taking in the wood. To see if there might be a connection. We would have to do it in the evening I suppose."

"Oh, that's why you look so scruffy, is it, Oldroyd? I had wondered if you were on permanent undercover duty." Merton said.

They all laughed.

"Yes. Great idea. Thanks. You'll need someone else. Firth. You two work together, do you?" The Central DCs nodded. "Good show. I'll leave that with you then. DC Harlow will give you the lowdown. Meanwhile, while Sergeant Harris is working out a strategy and hopefully making some appointments, Harlow will also give you a bit of a briefing on some of our overdue bread and butter work I'd like you to catch up on please."

"Everybody's got a job then. Busy day, busy week, I think. Let's hope it's a successful one. Unless anything crops up during the day, we'll compare notes at 0800 tomorrow." DI Merton concluded.

◆ ◆ ◆

It took Sergeant Harris over an hour of intensive phone calling to track down the telephone numbers and addresses of the Thursday Club members who were not yet known to them. With some, he made an appointment to visit. There were now only two he had so far been unable to reach. He would try again later.

Meanwhile, DC Harlow was acquainting DCs Firth and Oldroyd on several of Divisional CID's most significant outstanding cases together with a feel for the geography of the patch. He also filled them in with what he knew about the alleged illegal drugs activity in the woods and what the young lad, Pete, had said. It was agreed that it might be the best plan to leave a visit to the woods until Thursday evening, exactly a week after the murder and the activity which the young lad, Pete, had reported.

◆ ◆ ◆

DI Merton and Taylor had arrived at Margaret's house at about eleven o'clock. The small back room seemed full. Margaret was in her wheelchair in her usual corner. "Sometimes I manage to get onto the settee but usually it's easier to stay in this," she said. Merton and Taylor sat on dining chairs while Sarah and Geoffrey were on the settee. Sarah had made a pot of coffee and brought out some biscuits.

DI Merton was explaining how the investigation was going. "This kind of inquiry always takes some time while we gather lots of pieces of information and then hopefully we complete the puzzle. We haven't yet been able to speak to all of the people we want to. Sergeant Harris - you remember Sergeant Harris? - he and a colleague are out doing that now and we will be doing more later. It might take a few days."

Geoffrey who was clearly upset at the thought, said, "When can we bury Sally?"

"It's a matter for the Coroner first of all. We'll have to wait for that decision. Before that there's a matter of identification," Merton was saying.

Geoffrey was nodding, "It'll have to be me," he said, as though the dreadful knowledge had been permanently on his mind.

"Yes, we'll arrange that but it's all for a bit later. For now, we need your help quite a bit. We need to know more about who Sally was, something about her life, the people she knew, other than just the Thursday Club people. We know she worked at Armstrong's. She clearly spent a lot of time with you, Margaret. What did she do in the evenings and weekends? Did she meet people, go to any regular events, other than on Thursdays? Did she ever go on holiday?"

For a short while there was silence. Margaret

was collecting her thoughts. "It's all to do with me, isn't it? Sally has had to look after me all these years. If it hadn't been for me she would have had a very different life and she'd be alive now, wouldn't she? She couldn't leave me for more than a few hours. Sally was very good to me. I'm sure it was all because she felt so much guilt. She always thought she should have been in the front seat of the car instead of me. But she so much wanted to show off their new car and wanted me to sit in front to enjoy a drive in the country. Bill must have been killed instantly. I wish I had been …," she paused because those thoughts were never far from her mind. Graham got up and comforted her and she composed herself again.

Taylor said, "We're so sorry, Margaret, to be causing you upset, bringing these memories back. Can you help us a bit more though? Did Sally have any relationships with anybody … after the crash of course … at any time up to the present?"

Margaret and Geoffrey, sister and brother, looked at one another. They were silently exchanging thoughts. They imperceptibly nodded, as though coming to a mutual agreement about what to say.

Geoffrey answered, "For a few years after the crash, Sally was grieving really. We all were I suppose. It was so sad. Her leg healed up alright but she was having to learn how to look after Margaret. She really wanted to. She got everything ready for when Margaret came home from hospital. It was nearly a year while they did their best to put her spine right but her legs were never going to work. They weren't so clever with those kind of things as they are now. I was still around for a time but Sarah and me had already decided to live in London - that's where Sarah's from. I'd already got the job on the tube and we'd just bought a house. It would have been too difficult to go back on all that. Sally didn't seem to mind. She really wanted to do it.

"It was about that time I think that she started to go out regularly for a couple of hours or so. She said she went for a drink around the corner at the *George and Dragon.* On Thursdays it was. She had made some friends. It was only later she told us it was a darts team and she was quite good at it. We were pleased for her. Later on - just once in a while - say when me and Sarah had come back to visit for a weekend - Sally would go into town on a Saturday night, or even sometimes on another day. She went dancing. She'd always enjoyed that before ... Bill and her ... She said it really helped to get out once in a while. Obviously we could understand that, so we were pleased for her."

Graham paused and took a deep breath. He

looked at Margaret and there again was the imperceptible agreement.

"Then there was the day she came home and said she was pregnant."

There was another pause. "It was quite a shock. Difficult but somehow it worked out. We helped manage things. I had to be at work in London but Sarah came and stayed here a while. Sally had the baby. A little boy it was. She called him Timothy. Everyone rallied round but it was no use. What with Margaret and everything she just couldn't do it. Timothy was put up for adoption. They came to take him. It all happened quickly. One minute he was there and the next he was gone. A lovely little lad he was. Only knew him for about three months."

Taylor said quietly, "Is that the baby in the photograph in Sally's room?"

Graham nodded.

"Did Sally, did you, know who the father was?" asked Taylor.

Margaret replied, "Sally wouldn't say. Wouldn't talk about it. Flatly refused. She seemed to want to totally forget that bit of her life as though it had never happened. We asked her. We hoped the father might take some responsibility. Hardly any money coming in you see. It's always been a struggle but we've been careful and we've just managed. Graham couldn't afford being generous all the time."

"So she decided she needed a job. It had to be a bit flexible. She spoke to our neighbour, Mrs. Drummond - you've met her - and she said she would be able to come and see to me each day around dinner time. She was very good. So Sally got the job at Armstrong's. Nine till four, just four days a week, Tuesday to Friday. Sometimes she was able to come home in her lunch break for a few minutes. Only if need be. She was in the office. They understood and allowed Sally to come home if there was a real problem. But they wouldn't have wanted her to do that very often."

"That was all … how long ago? … around ten or eleven years ago by my reckoning," said DI Merton.

"Yes, about that," said Sarah. "I think Timothy will be about ten now."

"What about more recently?" asked Merton. 'Sally was still doing the same job, was she?" They nodded. "And was she still going out on Saturday nights?"

"Yes. A bit more often if anything, the last few years. Sometimes she went to the pictures. Not always just on Saturdays. These days, I seem to be able to manage for a bit longer so I was pleased for her that she could enjoy herself. I don't think she meant to but she once mentioned she went out with someone called Jim who was very nice. She got picked up at the corner of the street by this Jim.

DI Merton said, "Margaret, Graham, you're being a really big help. We hope that some of what you have said may help us bring Sally justice. Now, if you'll excuse me for just a minute, I've got to nip to the car. I'll be back in a jiffy."

◆ ◆ ◆

In the Rover, DI Merton switched on his pocket two-way radio and called up Divisional Control. "Please pass the following message to Detective Sergeant Harris as soon as possible - 'In recent years, Sally has been going out with someone called Jim - Juliet India Mike'. He will know what that means. Is that understood. Over?"

"Yes, all understood. Will do. Control over and out."

◆ ◆ ◆

Back in the small room, DI Merton didn't immediately sit down. He said, "just one more thing might help, if I may. DC Taylor here has already had a look in Sally's room. It's probably nothing at all but it does sometimes help us to get a rounded view of someone. That might help us understand why anyone would … er … do such a thing to her. I wonder if you'd mind if we went up and had another look? We won't disturb anything. A more experienced eye, you know," he smiled.

"That's fine, you know the way," Graham and Margaret said together.

In Sally's room, Taylor pointed out the nice clothes and jewellery and the two photographs on the walls which she and Harris had noted on Saturday. DI Merton opened the several drawers of the dressing table and had a careful look inside each one. In the bottom drawer he found a folder with some papers inside and quickly flipped through it. Underneath the folder, at the back of the drawer was a blue UK passport. It was Sally's, issued about five years earlier. Even though the photograph was without a smile he could see that she had been an attractive woman. What puzzled him, however, were several official border stamps, including French and Italian.

He opened the two doors of the wardrobe, took an even closer look at the clothes and then got down on his hands and knees, feeling towards the back of the wardrobe. At the back and just above the level of the hemlines of most of the dresses there was a shelf, probably for shoes. Indeed there were some shoes, hidden by the clothes. Also hidden, at the right hand end of the shelf, he found a shoe box. He brought it out and, carefully removing the lid, revealed several fat, unsealed, brown envelopes. Each one was packed with five pound or one pound notes. On top of the envelopes was a grey Post Office Savings Bank pass book. A brief look inside revealed a credit balance of more than £7,000. DI Merton flipped quickly through the pages and made a note of the account number in his pocket book. He showed Taylor and then carefully restored things as he had found them.

They took their leave, with thanks and promises to keep in touch with news.

"Well, said Merton as they returned to the Rover, "we can't justify another pub lunch can we? What have you got in your sandwiches?"

Taylor wasn't thinking about sandwiches. She was just amazed at the amount of money she had just seen. She said, "Shouldn't we have done something with that money. For safekeeping, maybe? Thousands of pounds altogether. What's it there for? And she only had a pound note and a few coins in her bag, didn't she?"

DI Merton said, "I reckon three or four thousand at a guess. Plus the bank book, as you say. It's not ours to do anything with, is it? At the moment we have no reason to believe it's the proceeds of crime. Margaret can't get upstairs. It's unlikely that Graham, or even Sarah, knows about it, otherwise they would either have had it out of there by now or would have been less willing for us to poke around."

"I wonder if she told anyone else about it," said Taylor.

"I doubt it. Margaret said it had been a struggle but they just managed. I think that money is Sally's little secret. Retirement fund, a better house one day maybe. Who knows? I wonder how she got it?"

After a few moments of thought, he added, "I am beginning to think that our Sally was quite a girl."

CHAPTER 13

Detective Inspector Merton's cheese and pickle sandwiches were the pre-packed affair in one of those new-fangled triangular plastic containers which he always struggled to open. He had picked them up that morning from his usual corner shop, together with a packet of cheese and onion crisps and a can of cola. Taylor had made her own ham salad ones and packed them into a Tupperware container, together with a tomato. She also had a flask of coffee.

Having driven out of Beech Street, turning left into Forest Road, they had parked facing the tall grey steel railings which surrounded Armstrong's factory. Now they sat having their lunch, thinking about Sally's life and all they had just heard.

Taylor spoke first. "Where do you think all that money came from, Sir?"

"John will do while we're out and about like this," he said. "Good question. Knowing where that cash came from could be the key to the whole thing. But we're some way off knowing just which lock that key will fit. And it may not be relevant at all."

"How do you mean?" Taylor asked.

"Something that should always be in the back of a detective's mind. Basic CID training. No doubt you'll be going on a course sometime soon. It's the reason for a lot of crime but it's also a crime in itself. Does that sound like an interesting conundrum, Taylor? Carol"

She thought about the conundrum for a few minutes. "Got it! Blackmail. Could that be it?"

"Well, never jump to conclusions too early but it's a possibility, don't you think?" Merton said. "When there's a lot of dosh involved. But she'd need to have had a hold over somebody to blackmail them. What about the father of that baby she had, years ago? She'd got the papers in that folder in the drawer - certificates, adoption documents and the like, copies I think - which she could use as a hold over someone.

"But I've been thinking of other ways she could have got that sum together. She should have put more of it in the bank though. Don't let any burglars know about it. Makes me nervous thinking of all that cash just sitting there. Margaret would be a sitting duck. When things are a bit clearer I might suggest they should do something about it. Anyway I'm rambling on. Helps me think.

"What other ways? Prostitution for one. She seems to have been a nice girl even though no longer young but this goes back some years probably. High class escort? Around here? She could have fitted it in some evenings, maybe. Nah. Not sure, with Margaret to look after. The only other way is, well, she went to work here at Armstrong's. Let's go and find out how much she got paid, shall we?"

They packed away the empty containers and Merton drove through a tall gate into Armstrong's yard, parking in a space neatly marked 'Visitors'. They entered the modern building into a pristine area labelled 'Reception'. An older, grey haired woman sat at the reception desk and seemed to know who they were and what they wanted.

"You're the police, aren't you? I'll get Mr. Armstrong." She spoke into an intercom and just a moment later a small grey haired man emerged through a door.

"Hello," he said. "I'm Armstrong, Colin Armstrong, Managing Director. It's about Sally isn't it? Wondered if you might come here. We didn't know what to do since we heard about it. Terrible. Oh, you've met my wife. She's had to look after reception since …."

DI Merton introduced himself and Taylor. Warrant cards were shown and hands were shaken.

"What can I do for you? Anything to help." Mr Armstrong said.

"Would you mind if we used your office please?" asked Merton.

"But, er, yes of course," said Armstrong, leading the way through the door into a small office.

"Hope you don't mind that, Sir." Merton said. "A bit public out there."

"We're not very busy at the moment. Customers have got almost all the boxes they need for the Christmas trade. Have to wait till the new year now for things to pick up. Had to lay a few people off."

"Had Sally worked for you very long?" asked Merton.

"We were only trying to work that out this morning. Must be eight or nine years at least. She was good at her job. You know, reception, phone, a bit of filing and so on. My wife Muriel has had to step in. You met her? Of course … you just did. Silly. It's all a bit of a shock. Muriel's a

Director too. She doesn't normally have to work here. We'll have to sort out what to do about that. Maybe after Christmas."

"Apart from work," Merton said, "Did you know Sally socially in any way? Outside work I mean. Any common interest, clubs, that kind of thing?"

Armstrong looked a bit shocked. "No. Didn't really know her at all, other than at work of course. Socially? We tried a staff Christmas party a couple of years but they weren't very well attended so we didn't carry on with them."

"Do you know anything about the Thursday Club, Mr. Armstrong?"

"Thursday Club? No. Never heard of it. What ....?"

At that moment there was a very sudden and very loud high pitched noise which disappeared within seconds. It had seemed to shake the building.

"What was that?" asked Merton, taking his hands away from his ears.

"Oh, we get them sometimes," said Armstrong. "Jets from the RAF base. Training. Usually in pairs. They're not really supposed to fly over the town but it happens sometimes. We get used to it. Now, what was it you said? Thursday Club? No, not heard of it." Armstrong was beginning to look a bit anxious, for no apparent reason. "Should I have? What is it? What's it got to do with Sally?"

"Mr. Armstrong," said DI Merton. "We won't keep you much longer but there's one last thing. I understand you pay wages on Fridays. I think you still pay in cash. Obviously, Sally didn't come in on Friday so you will presumably still have her pay packet. May I see it please?"

Armstrong looked even more anxious but probably only because this detective seemed to know more than he expected him to. He said, "Well, yes. We're going to have to account for it. Not sure how we do that yet. With the Inland Revenue and all that, I mean. Get a refund of tax. A bit unusual."

"May I see the packet please, Sir?" said Merton quite firmly.

"I'm not sure that's the right thing to do ... that we should be doing ... confidential ... Oh, well, yes. Just a minute." Armstrong had become flustered and hesitant but he went through a different door and could be heard talking to someone. A few minutes went by and he returned with a small, brown envelope which he handed to Merton.

"Just checking, Mr. Armstrong," said Merton,

looking at it. "Tell me, am I right that the money in this pay packet is the money due to Sally Weston for work she has already done and which she would normally have collected from you last Friday. Is that correct?"

"Well, yes, that's right." said Armstrong with an air of defeat.

"In that case, you will be pleased to know that I am going to save you a lot of bother with all that accounting with the Inland Revenue and I am going to take the packet and ensure that Sally's sister Margaret gets it in due course. You know about her sister, do you?" Armstrong nodded and appeared to want to protest but then thought better of it. Merton continued, "Don't worry, we'll give you a receipt." He nodded at Taylor who got a pad from her shoulder bag and issued the receipt which she gave to Armstrong.

"Thank you for your help, Sir. We're done for now but we may want to speak to you again. Goodbye."

He and Taylor left the building briskly, leaving Armstrong open mouthed. They nodded to Mrs. Armstrong as they passed the reception desk.

As they got into the car Taylor noticed that her boss was in a bit uptight. "What's up, Sir?" she asked.

DI Merton turned the car and headed it, a bit too fast, for Divisional HQ.

"I'm sure you must have noticed, Taylor. Armstrong obviously knew that Sally had been murdered but not once did he ask how it had happened or how the investigation was going. Nor did he ask about how Sally's sister was managing. He must have known about her situation because apparently Sally had been given a bit of flexibility in the hours she worked. All he was bothered about was how to account for Sally's un-issued wages to the Inland Revenue. We've saved him that bother. On top of all that, Sally was being paid a pittance. Talk about Scrooge. It's no wonder nobody wanted to go to his Christmas parties. Probably had to take their own bottle. And he lays people off just before Christmas. Nice. Cardboard boxes … bah!"

"By the way," he continued, handing Taylor the wage packet, "put that in an evidence bag and book it in. You never know if it might be needed as evidence at some stage."

"Maybe Colin Armstrong has got a lot of worries on his mind, Sir," said Taylor.

❖ ❖ ❖

"So, how was your day, Sergeant Harris, DC Harlow? Hopefully some useful news?"

It was now mid-afternoon. The team was back in the CID office although the Central DCs, Firth and Oldroyd, hadn't yet returned.

DS Harris explained, "Well, Sir, I spent some time with directories and on the phone this morning and I think we've now got a pretty good list of the Thursday Club members and their addresses and phone numbers. I've added all those details to the list on the board."

DI Merton studied the board for a minute or so, then nodded his approval. "Very good. I think we need some different coloured pins in the map showing where each of the people we know about lives, not just the Thursday Club ones. Taylor, if you would, please."

Taylor found enough green pins for the Thursday Club members. She also put in a yellow pin for 66 Beech Street because of Sally's brother and sister-in-law. In her mind, only theoretically, they could be suspects. They seemed a bit defensive. A fanciful idea? But could they possibly have killed Sally and were biding their time to take the money from her wardrobe? Graham had said he had been at home in Finchley on Thursday night.

Surely not? Not family. They would end up having to look after Margaret. Taylor kept her counsel. She was learning there were so many small details in a case like this. Being a detective was almost entirely about working out which ones mattered.

She pushed another yellow pin firmly into the map where Armstrong's factory was shown and another into where the wood was represented in dark green at about the site of the hollowed out tree, the alleged hang out of drug taking youths. That pin was almost touching the red pin representing the murder site.

Harlow said, "I gave the Central lads the messages for a few of what I thought were the more urgent outstanding cases and also passed on Taylor's thoughts about the link between the Tallows and the 'Second Chance' shop in Millwood. Hope that was okay? And they've got a map. They seemed happy enough. No doubt they'll report soon, Sir."

As an afterthought he added, "Oh yes, I got hold of the Met Office. Very helpful they were. They've just phoned back. It was definitely heavy cloud over Millwood last Tuesday and Wednesday evenings and overnight."

"Good show," Merton said, "Did you get to see anybody today, Harris?"

"Right, Sir," said DS Harris. "I made some appointments and we went to see two of them this afternoon. They're the ones who live in the same street ... Dover Avenue. The first was Fred Mellor - you and Richard saw him the other day - and then Tom Freestone. I tried to get to see the other one who lives near them, in Brighton Crescent. That's Jim Wheatland. I gather he's in business. I wonder if he's something to do with the brewery? Couldn't get an answer but then I got your message and thought it might be an idea to hang on and knock on his door this evening, maybe."

"Yes," Merton said, thoughtfully. "I'm interested in this Jim after what we heard, and saw, at Margaret's this morning. That right Taylor?" Taylor agreed.

"Then," said DS Harris, "from Fred Mellor's we went just up the road, on the other side, to see Mr. Freestone. Tom Freestone. He's pleasant enough but he's one of these people who is always on the go. Never sits still for more than a couple of minutes. If you remember, he's the one who arrived at the *George and Dragon* late on Thursday - didn't get a game of darts - because he had to go and repair his mother's washing machine. He had a swift half pint in the bar and then he left with Jim, in Jim's car. He says that would have been around a quarter to ten. He remembers that Sally had already left a few minutes before. He says he has no knowledge or anything to do with Sally other than at the Thursday Club. To be honest, Sir - gut feeling - I can't see either Fred or Tom having anything to do with this."

"Right, thanks Harris. I agree with you on

Fred and I'm sure you're right on Tom," said DI Merton. "Taylor, put a pencil line through those two. And while you're at it you can do the same with the Lowesbys. Taylor and I were reasonably happy with them yesterday. Leave Norman Wilson for a bit. So, four down and seven Thursday Club members to go. We'll include Bruce Morgan for completeness. Plus anyone else in the frame."

Just then, DCs Firth and Oldroyd, came into the office. "Hope you've had a successful day?" asked Merton.

"We think we have, hopefully," DC Oldroyd replied. "We've called on a few of the more outstanding usual break-ins, domestics and, oh yes, a dog theft. Taken statements and put them in the system. As part of that we had a drive through Millwood and had a look at Beech Street. That seems to be where all the action is at the moment. DC Harlow told us about Taylor's linking the scrap merchant - Tallow - with the second hand shop in town. We had a look and agree and wondered if a search warrant for Tallow's place might be a good idea, Sir?"

"You think there might be a stash of silver and jewellery at Tallow's place do you?" asked DI Merton.

Taylor chipped in and reiterated her suspicions about the yellow signs and the Bedford lorry. She added, "Even the guy in the shop and the son who came to the door when we first called on them looked as if they could be related. Brothers maybe. Height, build, facial features and so on."

DI Merton thought for a moment. "If you're going to search that rat hole of a place, good luck. But you'll need to get on with it. Yes - get your search warrant and do it tomorrow. You'll need some uniform boots on the ground to help because we're all pretty tied up. I'll have a word with Archie Johnson. Oh yes. Why not go along with them, Taylor? You set it up. See it through to a result, with a bit of luck. Good experience. The rest of us are only going to be talking to Thursday Club members."

Taylor was pleased. "Yes, Sir." she said.

"Thank you, Sir," said DC Oldroyd. "We're pretty used to setting up this sort of thing in Central Division. Routine really. There's one more thing. We're going to be even busier tomorrow because we've also decided to have a wander into the wood around 2000 hours to see if there's anyone there up to no good. Not just the drugs thing but we would test the water about the murder, too. Probably nothing in that though, as you said, Sir. We decided on tomorrow because the weather forecast's at least dry and not too cold. If it comes to nothing we'll try again on Thursday because that's the day the boy said he saw people going into to the wood last week."

"I like your style," DI Merton said. I take it you've no homes to go to? But thanks anyway chaps. You're being a big help."

"Now to tonight," he continued, "Sergeant Harris, I'll meet you at the *George and Dragon* at 1800 hours. I'll be in the bar, no doubt having a snack and chatting up the barmaid. You can as well if you want. Have a snack, I mean. Then we'll go and talk to Jim Wheatland if he's at home. I'm not taking you Taylor because people will start talking." He grinned. "No, I think this Jim fella might have something to tell us and it may need a bit of experience to help winkle it out. We'll see. "That alright, Harris?"

"Fine, Sir. The *George and Dragon* bar at 1800 it is." DS Harris was also grinning.

"So, we'll be back as usual tomorrow morning. No doubt we'll have some interviews lined up to keep us busy. Good night all."

❖ ❖ ❖

Geoffrey Smith, landlord at the *George and Dragon*, opened the doors at six o'clock. A few minutes later DI Merton and DS Harris walked into the bar, using the door from the car park. The young woman behind the bar greeted them, "Good evening. The policemen return."

She was an experienced barmaid who knew her customers - a great asset to any public house.

"Good evening," said Merton and, guessing, he said, "Are you Lucy by any chance?"

"Touché," said Lucy. "Good guess but I'm here most evenings so not too difficult. And sometimes Sunday lunchtime for the lunches. You were here yesterday. What can I get you gentlemen?"

"We pay our own way, don't we Harris? Makes life less argumentative. Not on expenses today. Mine's a pint of bitter. Your usual shandy, Harris? What's on the bar menu, Lucy?"

"We don't do bar meals on Mondays. Never very busy and it's Chef's day off." Lucy was pulling the beers. "But there's sandwiches and our ploughman's suppers are legendary."

They agreed on a ploughman's each. "You'll know we're making inquiries about what happened last Thursday, Lucy? Did anything out of the ordinary happen here on Thursday evening?"

"We can't get over it," said Lucy. "Sally ... poor Sally. She was lovely. Been coming here a long time ... on Thursdays. Just Thursdays. Can't understand why anyone would ... why was she there ... in the wood? Oh, sorry. Anything unusual on Thursday, you said? You mean ... the darts people ... surely not. Well, no, not really. It was the darts team. They played darts, enjoyed themselves as usual."

"Well, we have to consider every possibility," said Harris, "it helps us to understand what happened if we know where everyone was, who might have seen something. That kind of thing. Can you remember the Club members leaving? Who followed who? Anything you can remember might be helpful."

"Let me think. Fred always leaves first, about as soon as the match is over. He must be about the oldest of them. He doesn't hang around chatting much. Usually the next ones are the ones with cars. Perhaps they have a way to go. Ray and Janet and … whatsisname … er …?"

"Is that Rob?" suggested DS Harris, eyeing the ploughman's which Geoffrey had just brought in.

Geoffrey greeted them, "Everything OK?"

"Fine, thanks, Mr. Smith," said Merton. "Just a few more inquiries. You not very busy?"

"Monday. There'll be a few along in a bit. Excuse me, I'll just put another log or two on the fire."

"I've been thinking about Thursday," said Lucy. "Kept me awake thinking about poor Sally. The ladies usually go at about the same time. So when Janet and Ray go, Sally usually left just a bit later. I don't think she has far to go … sorry, used to have far to go. Now, let me think. Then there was Dylan and Bruce. They usually go around the same time. I think they live near one another. Probably walk back home together. It was cold though, wasn't it? Brrrr. But on Thursday, oh yes, Bruce was talking to somebody, Jim, that's it. So he followed Dylan out a few minutes later and no doubt caught him up. Funny how you can remember things if you try, isn't it?"

"It's really helpful, Lucy. A good bit of cheddar this," said Harris.

"Yes, that's it," went on Lucy. Tom was in his usual rush. He'd arrived late and he wasn't here long. Went out with Jim. I think he sometimes gets a lift with him. Norman stayed on for a bit. He's often in here anyway. He's only across the road."

"You said Norman stayed on longer than the others?" asked Merton.

"Yes, I'm pretty sure he did on Thursday. He often does. You see that comfy chair over there by the fire? That's his usual place and I'm sure I saw him in it. For some reason it gets busier in the bar after 9.30 so, well, yes. I'm pretty sure."

"You didn't see him leave or maybe get up and go out, maybe to the gents, and come back again or anything like that?" said Merton.

"I can't really remember. He'd certainly gone by 10.30 though. Well before that, I think."

A group of customers came in just then and Lucy went to serve them.

Merton and Harris finished their suppers and returned to the car park. The lights on the rear wall of the pub lit up the nearest cars quite well but beyond that it was very dark.

"If anybody walked down that footpath, the other side of the fence, said Merton, "would you be able to see them?"

"Yes. If you were looking that way. You'd see their heads over the fence and they'd be in view for a short while until they got about half way along, towards the wood," replied Harris. "Especially if there was a full moon."

"Mmm." replied Merton. "Let's go."

◆ ◆ ◆

Jim Wheatland had not had a good day at the office. There had been one problem after another, especially with getting up to speed with the Christmas trade. He was one of the three Wheatland brothers who had inherited the Wheatland Brewery in Market Easterby more than 30 years ago. For Jim, then still in his late twenties, that had been perfect timing, as it solved the problem of what he should do when he left the RAF just after the War. Gradually the young brothers had got the hang of running the business. Now the brewery had become very successful indeed.

The problems of the day, mainly involving the extra supplies needed at this time of year, had gone on and on. That meant he had arrived home later than usual and not in the best of moods. It wasn't his usual demeanour by any means. He enjoyed his self-imposed freedom of being a foot-loose and fancy-free bachelor. He very much enjoyed the company of attractive, mature, available women with whom he endeavoured to share a good time. Those women had the pleasure of being in the good company of a mature, handsome man with a fat wallet. Jim had never seen any reason to get tangled up in a marriage. He was enjoying the kind of life which can be lived when you don't have to worry about money.

Jim Wheatland's large, mature house and gardens are situated in the exclusive, tree-lined Brighton Crescent in south-west Millwood. Its semi-circular gravel drive links the two entrances. At long last, after the 35-minute drive from the office, Jim's red MG two-seater sports car had crunched up the drive and stopped facing the double garage. "I'll put it away in a bit," he was thinking as he opened the front door of the house and switched on a few lights. In the front lounge, he dumped his briefcase on a side table and poured himself a sizeable neat single malt Laphroaig and sat in his comfortable chair. He would get himself a sandwich or something a bit later.

The whisky was helping him wind down and the trials of the day were slowly receding. Twenty minutes or so went by and the clock showed it was 7.20pm. He was thinking he should really get himself a bit of something for his tea. He hoped Mrs. Hobson, his part-time housekeeper, had done the shopping he had asked her to do.

All of a sudden he realised he had barely thought about Sally all day, what with everything going on. Before this morning, especially over the weekend, he had thought of little else but her and what had happened.

The headlights of a car shone brightly through the window as a car came into the drive, curving around and stopping outside the front door. The headlights were switched off, a few moments went by and the door chimes sounded.

Jim sighed. He certainly wasn't expecting anyone. He opened the front door.

"Good evening, Sir. Is it Mr. Wheatland?" said the older of the two men standing there.

"Who wants to know?" said Jim, always cautious, although actually realising who these two men were likely to be. Rob had phoned him yesterday and they had had a long talk about what might have happened. They had speculated that the police would want to talk to the Thursday Club members.

"Sorry to disturb your evening, Sir. We are police officers, just making inquiries. I am DI Merton and this is DS Harris." They displayed their warrant cards.

"Yes, of course. About Sally, is it?" said Jim. "You'd better come in.

In the lounge he said, "Please, have a seat. It's been a stonker of a day. I've just got in. Having a quick snifter. Care to join me?"

"Thank you for the offer but no thank you," DI Merton said. "In fact, we've just sampled your product, I think, at the *George and Dragon.* It is Wheatlands Brewery, isn't it, Sir?"

Jim laughed. "Caught me out. Not difficult is it. Name's everywhere. Up to our ears at the minute though. Start of the Christmas build up. Yes, I'm one of the directors of Wheatlands Brewery. This is about Sally presumably? Thursday night and all that? Can't really take it all in."

DS Harris said, "You were at the *George and Dragon* last Thursday evening, Sir?"

As the Sergeant spoke, Jim noticed that the

tone had now become serious. "Well, yes I was. Thursday Club. Darts. Just about every Thursday. Amazing we're still doing it really, after all these years."

"All these years, Sir?" Harris asked. DI Merton had stood up and was slowly wandering around the big lounge, looking at some photographs which were displayed in frames on a side table and on the walls. Many were black and white pictures of wartime aeroplanes.

While wondering what Merton was doing Jim said, "Yes. Must be about 30 years. How can it be that long? Six of us to start with. Knew each other on the air base. Wartime. Left about the same time and we just carried on meeting up …"

"Yes," interrupted DS Harris, perpetuating the serious nature of the matter, "the little get-togethers carried on and grew and eventually there was the darts team and the darts league and you met every Thursday evening at the *George and Dragon*. That's about right isn't it, Sir?"

DI Merton had sat down again. He and Harris were a good double act. Harris had demonstrated the seriousness of the inquiry. Now Merton asked, "Your Wartime service. What were you doing?"

Jim relaxed a little. "I was a pilot. Spitfires usually, earlier on. Reconnaissance mostly. Some activity. Managed to bring a few of the others down. Long time ago now. Still good to meet up with Bruce and Rob on Thursdays. Rob was one of the mechanics. Kept us flying despite everything. We had to trust him, didn't we? Bruce was in the technical department ... photographic. All of it was equally important stuff. There's only the three of us old originals in the Club left now. We're good mates."

"As you've appreciated, Sir," said Merton, we're here making inquiries about Sally Weston's murder. Yes, it is a terrible business. So, at the moment we need to talk to everybody who knew her to try to understand what happened to her after she left the bar at the *George and Dragon* and why anybody would want to harm her."

Jim was nodding. "Yes, I can see that. I suppose all of us at the Thursday Club are obvious people to speak to and that's why you're here. But I really can't see why any of us would know much. We all thought Sally was lovely. She was one of us." With his background, Jim Wheatland had a straight back and a stiff upper lip and so wasn't the emotional type. But it was noticed that he came close to it then.

"And she was a good darts player, I understand?" said Merton. Jim nodded.

"Just so that we get a picture of everyone's movements last Thursday evening, what time did you leave the pub?" asked DS Harris.

"Oh, goodness. Let me think. Most of them had gone. Yes, Tom had come in late in a bit of a rush. He just called in to check up on the arrangements for next week, no, this week now, Thursday. It's an important league game. If it goes ahead now. Yes, Tom just had half a pint. Norman was sitting by the fire. He would have been the last to go. I gave Tom a lift home - I often do - I pass his house, just down the road. So I'm guessing we had left by a quarter to ten."

"How long does it take you to drive home?" persisted DS Harris.

"Oooh, only about three or four minutes I should think. A bit longer if the traffic lights in the Square are on red, maybe."

DI Merton stepped in, "Did you know anything of Sally other than at the Thursday Club. Do you know what any of her other interests were. Her home life and so on?"

"Well, she lived in Beech Street. Don't know the number. She looked after her sister who's in a wheelchair. It was in a road accident a long time ago, apparently. Sally's husband was killed. She never re-married."

DI Merton realised Jim Wheatland seemed to know more about Sally than any of the others had done so far. He leaned forward and looked straight at Jim and said, "You'll appreciate that this is a murder inquiry, Mr. Wheatland, so I have to be a little persistent and I need to know the whole story. I have to ask you, did you have any relationship with Sally Weston other than at the Thursday Club? Bear in mind that I have noticed a photograph on your sideboard over there which, I am pretty sure, looks like you and Sally on a dance floor."

After a moment's thought while he took a sip from his glass, Jim sighed and resigned himself to telling the story. "It was about seven or eight years ago. I asked Sally if she would like to come out with me. Everybody always thought she seemed a bit jolly, you know, life and soul of the party. She knew that all the guys loved her and she played up to that, all in a perfectly innocent way, as far as I knew. But I wasn't quite convinced. I thought it was a bit of bravado and she was quite sad really. That's why I asked her out. She didn't say yes right away. She had to think about it. That was when she told me about her sister Margaret and said she couldn't stay out late. Anyway, just occasionally, we would spend an evening together. I picked her up at the end of her street by the phone box because she said she didn't want to be seen being picked up in a posh car, as she called it. We would go for a meal or just a drink."

Jim took another sip from his glass.

"Presumably you went dancing at some stage?" asked Merton

"That came later, after a few months. She told me she was out of practice because her leg - she'd broken it in the car crash - had taken time to heal. She wanted to see how she got on with it, dancing I mean. So, some Saturday nights we went out dancing, yes, and we both enjoyed it. Maybe once a month. Couldn't stay out late though."

"Would that have been to the Palais de Dance in town?" asked Merton.

"Yes, how did you know?"

"There was a membership card in her handbag," said Merton, "and one for the Starlight Club too."

"That was only recent. Not so far to go, Lupton. We decided to give it a try."

"Did Sally ever come here, to your house, Sir?" asked Merton.

"Look, Inspector," Jim began, now beginning to sound a bit annoyed with the questioning, "I am a bachelor. Never wanted it any other way. But, sure, I like the company of nice women from time to time. Come to think of it, they quite like my company, too. Sally knew all about that and yes, she came here sometimes. Over the years, there have even been a few occasions when

Sally's brother and his wife have come up from London where they live and they've taken Margaret on a short holiday. It worked out very well because it gave Sally a break and we could have a weekend away as well. Maybe Paris, Rome, even Brighton."

There must have been a look in Sergeant Harris's face because Jim went on, "Okay, if you like Sergeant, a dirty weekend away. There's no shame in that. We are … were … consenting adults. Both free to do as we liked. Is any of that helping your inquiries Inspector? All I can say is that I have been thinking about Sally every minute since I found out about … about … what happened to her. I'll miss her a lot."

DI Merton allowed a few moments to pass. He said, "I have to ask this. Please don't misunderstand. There is an important reason for the question. Was there ever any money - in cash - involved between you and Sally?"

Even Sergeant Harris was wondering where this was going because he wasn't yet aware of what DI Merton and Taylor had found in Sally's bedroom.

Jim Wheatland sighed and said, a bit angrily, "You're thinking she was some kind of prostitute aren't you? No, you're wrong. Very wrong. There wasn't anything like that at all. As I said, Sally was restricted about how long she could go out for, because of her sister. She told me all about it soon after we first started going out together and she said the work she did at that factory near where she lives - Armstrong's isn't it - didn't pay her much. She even showed me her pay packet once. She couldn't change jobs because she had to be near home. Nothing else would pay any more. Anyway, to cut a long story short, I gave her some money one time. Not a lot. But over the years, looking after Margaret cost more and more. Her brother helped a bit, I think. There wasn't much in benefits. So I helped as much as I could because we liked to be together. I was pleased to do it because I valued Sally's company. I like to think it was helping to keep their heads above water. As you can imagine, I'm not short of a bob or two. No, Inspector Merton, Sally was certainly not a prostitute."

"Okay, thank you for being frank. I understand," said DI Merton. "Sorry to pursue this. As I say, it is important. What sort of sums were involved in this, er generosity of yours."

"It was probably a tenner or twenty pound note every so often to begin with but in the last few years I made it a more regular, monthly arrangement. Fifty pounds. As I say, it's petty cash for me but I am sure it made all the difference to Sally and her sister. I only regret never meeting Margaret. I'm sure she's a lovely lady. Maybe I should go to see her and see if there's anything I can do. I'm sure she never knew about the money. I don't think Sally wanted her to know anyone was supporting her like that. In any case I didn't mind because Sally was a really good friend."

"I think that will be all for now, thank you, Mr. Wheatland. It's been a very helpful chat. We may want to talk to you again. By the way, will you be at the *George and Dragon* this Thursday evening?" said DI Merton.

"I haven't heard anything about that from the others so far. One or two of them might not want to do it but I think we should carry on. It is a league game on Thursday. We should do it in remembrance of Sally," said Jim.

"Thank you. Sorry to keep you so long. Good night, Sir."

◆ ◆ ◆

DI Merton and DS Harris were back in the car. Merton said, "No, of course it wasn't prostitution. It was blackmail. Except the victim was very happy to be blackmailed and hadn't got a clue that he was being blackmailed. Well, that's the way I see it", said Merton.

"Yes, Sir," said Harris, "But how can that be? Sally hadn't got anything tangible over him, had she? How could it be called blackmail?"

"You don't think so, Harris?" Merton said. "I think Sally had quite a lot on offer - in the bedroom department, you know, which our Jim wouldn't have wanted to lose and that he was happy to keep paying for. You can call it prostitution if you like but I agree with you so far, Harris. I can't think of any law that she's fallen foul of."

> Merton paused a moment, then said, "A very clever girl was our Sally. Clearly a bit too clever for her own good."

CHAPTER 14

"Now then team, a slight change of plan today." DI Merton was addressing the detectives in the CID office, first thing on Tuesday morning.

"Is everything set up for your raid on Tallows?" he asked.

DC Oldroyd responded, "Our guess is that the Tallows have no set schedule and probably get up late. We didn't think a dawn raid was warranted for this one so it's all set up for 1000 hours. A van full of uniform down the street ready to go in and a couple of them in a panda keeping a distant eye on the second hand shop and the lorry for an hour or so and to report if there's any movement. We don't want any surprises".

"Right," said DI Merton. "Well done for getting that set up. The change I'm going to make is because there's just three DCs involved in this. Very good too, I'm sure - although one is a squeaky clean new DC. So I'm giving you Sergeant Harris as well. Can't have you having it all your own way, while the cat's away, without a bit of supervision. Any problems? No. Good."

"So, Sergeant Harris has also kindly set up a couple of appointments for today for DC Harlow and myself to concentrate on …"

The phone on Merton's desk rang. He picked it up. "Good morning, Sir. Yes it is good to be a bit warmer. Yes, quite busy, Sir. Plenty to do but a good team. Making progress. Yes. Still a few interviews. Doing those today. Hopefully pulling all the threads together tomorrow. We'll know more then. I'll keep you informed. Yes, Sir, all being well by Friday. Yes. Good morning, Sir."

"Detective Superintendent Briggs looking for results as usual. Why not? We are too, aren't we?" said Merton. "Let's get going."

◆ ◆ ◆

After the four involved with the raid had left the office, DI Merton and DC Harlow remained. "No action for us today then, Harlow. Just talking, eh?" Merton said.

"Suits me, Sir," Harlow replied, still retaining that image of Sally's post mortem, "I just want to get Sally's killer."

"Good man," said Merton. "Maybe today we'll

come up with the key to the mystery. We're probably already looking at it but can't quite see it. Any ideas?"

"Like you said, Sir, the puzzle for me is why was she killed just there? Why would she go down that path and through the gap in the fence? To meet somebody there? Even if it was moonlit. Did she go there with someone? Or was it just some random encounter? All I know is I want to get the bastard."

"Agreed," said Merton. "Shall we go?"

In the Rover, they followed the road to Millwood, turning right along the straight road which passed the airfield on the left with its high wire fence. In about a mile, at the end of the fence, they turned left following the sign to Morton. Just before they came to the village they passed the main gate into RAF Millwood. There was a substantial gate house, red and white lifting barriers and signs displaying "Alert Level High". Two guards in RAF uniform were visible, carrying rifles.

"They're taking this Cold War business seriously, aren't they?" DC Harlow said.

DI Merton was concentrating on finding the first address they needed in the village. Having found it and parked the car, they walked up the short path to a neat, modest house with many rose bushes in the front garden. The door was answered by a woman wearing an apron and drying her hands on a towel.

"Yes?" the woman said sharply, probably thinking they were salesmen.

"Sorry to disturb you, Madam. We're police officers." They went through the drill of introducing themselves and displaying their identities. "We're hoping to be able to speak to Mr. Robert Jordan. He may be expecting us."

"He's in the shed. Always tinkering. Do you want to come in? Just go in there. I'll fetch him."

They were shown into the small front room. There were several black and white pictures of wartime aeroplanes, airfield buildings and groups of airmen displayed on the walls.

"I'm guessing it's about Sally," said Robert Jordan as he came into the room. He was a slightly bent, older man with grey hair and sporting a fine handlebar moustache.

"Good morning, Mr. Jordan. Yes, we're investigating what happened to Sally Weston and we need to speak to everyone who knew her, including members of the Thursday Club. I understand you've already spoken to Sergeant Harris at the mobile police station?"

"Rob. Call me Rob. Yes, that's right. I wanted

to know how things were going. Nasty business. A real shock. Don't think it's quite sunk in yet. We won't see her again. We'll all miss her. Lovely lady. What do you want to know?"

"Well, we need to know when each of the Thursday Club members left the bar at the *George and Dragon* last week. It helps us to piece together what might have happened. When did you leave, Rob?"

"I didn't hang about last Thursday. Sharp frost. Didn't want to be late. Ray and Janet left and I think I was only two or three minutes after them. Most of the rest were still there but they're all in walking distance. No, hang on, Jim's car was still in the car park. Can't miss his red MG. He had his windscreen covered in a blanket. I should have thought of that but it was an early frost this year. Took me by surprise. Ray and Janet were still scraping their windscreen."

"Whereabouts in the car park were you parked, Rob?" Merton asked.

"My usual place. Nearly always anyway. Over by the fence at the far side. Seems safest there, away from people coming and going by the entrance, shunting about for spaces when it gets busy."

"You passed by Ray and Janet Lowesby then - on the way to your car? Or did you use the side entrance onto the footpath?"

"No. Used the door from the hallway. Needed the gents first. Before driving out here. You never know, do you, after a couple of pints? Oh, shouldn't have said that should I?" Rob grinned a bit sheepishly. "So, yes, I said goodnight to Ray and Janet. As I say, they were still clearing their windscreen."

"I'd like you to think back very carefully, Mr. Jordan, to when you were in the car park, walking to your car, passing Jim's car and the Lowesby's, saying good night to them and, presumably having to scrape your windscreen as well. Did you see anyone else?" DI Merton was speaking steadily and clearly.

"Nobody else in the car park but there was a couple walked down the footpath. Only saw them briefly out of the corner of my eye - just their heads over the fence - because I was trying to get my windscreen clear. Very hard frost. I don't use that de-icer spray stuff. I think it gums up the works. I had my back to the footpath scraping the windscreen. Took me at least ten minutes. It was cold. I like to do it thoroughly."

"Were the couple walking away from the pub or towards it?"

"Definitely away from the pub. You can only see heads going by over the fence. Probably wouldn't have noticed at all if the moon hadn't been so bright. A long time since I've seen a moon like that." said Rob.

"Think carefully, Rob, did you recognise who they were? Did you hear them talking?"

At that moment, Rob began to see that what he was telling these police officers might be important. He thought very hard and shook his head. Eventually he said, "No, sorry. Could that be important? Never thought about that. I don't even know where the footpath goes to, with not living in Millwood."

"Yes, it could be important to know who those two people were. Any clue at all, hair colour, hat, scarf, voices, tall, short ..."

Realisation was gaining pace in Rob's head and, having taken its time, now became instantly complete. Rob went quiet and pale. His mind was racing. Could he have been the one person to see Sally being taken to her death by her murderer? "But ... do you think ... no ... surely ..." He was trying to put that thought into words but words failed him.

DC Harlow had not spoken so far. He was appreciating how expertly his boss had gently but firmly, step by step, extracted valuable information from Rob who had not even been aware of having it before. He resolved to remember and learn from the experience.

He decided to play a part and said, "Rob, Sir, you can take it easy. The whole experience has been a bit of a shock to everyone, hasn't it? I wonder if Mrs. Jordan would be willing to make us a cup of tea?"

Rob nodded and left the room, returning a moment later. "Yes, Pat will bring it in."

Rob was still silently trying to force his memory to come up with that vital missing bit of information. At the time he hadn't given a single thought to who the couple on the footpath might be. Why would he? It had certainly never once entered his head that, if it had been Sally walking along that footpath, her companion might be someone that he knew. Surely, none of his friends could possibly ... the awful thought that he alone might hold that vital piece of information was beginning to trouble him.

As Rob's wife brought in a tray of tea mugs, DI Merton, thinking a distraction was necessary, asked Rob about his RAF service, pointing out some of the pictures on the wall.

Rob was pleased to have the distraction and responded to the interest. "Yes. Wartime of course. Not easy. I was an aircraft mechanic at the base. But we had some good times. Six of us got together afterwards and stayed in touch.

Eventually it became the Thursday Club ... oh, I suppose you already know all about that." He paused. "I guess you're wondering about the moustache. Usually it's for pilots and of course I was clean shaven while I was serving. But afterwards, well, I just decided to see if I could grow one because I had always quite fancied being a pilot. So, it's still here. Don't think Pat's very keen though." He smiled for a moment.

DI Merton was not rushing, allowing Rob's mind to perhaps recall any additional fraction of information about that couple walking along the footpath. They were all silently sipping tea.

"One of them was quite a bit taller than the other," Rob had put his mug down and rushed the information out. "One of them, only just see the top of their head above the fence. The other, all of their head showing. Wish I had taken more notice. Only seen them out of the corner of my eye. Didn't give them a thought. You know, likely to be locals just going home from the pub."

"It's okay," DI Merton said. "what you have told us is very valuable. It would be helpful, while we are out here, if you would give us a short written statement please. Just where you were, when you left the pub, what you were doing in the car park and what you saw. Okay, thanks. DC Harlow will do that with you."

The statement took about ten minutes to

write and sign. Merton said, "Here is my card. If anything else occurs to you - absolutely anything - give me a call. They'll take a message."

Getting up from the chair to leave, Merton thanked Mrs. Jordan for their teas and he said to Rob, "Can you point us in the right direction to where Adrian Cranmer lives?"

"Yes," said Rob. "Easy. You can almost see his house from here. I'll show you. But he's not there at the moment. We normally go together on Thursdays, to the Club, but he's got one of these new-fangled time share things in Spain. He was there last week and I think he'll be back this weekend. He usually goes for two weeks, about three times a year. Lucky devil."

Back in the Rover, they drove around to Adrian Cranmer's address, just to look at his house. Amazing what can be learned just by looking at where someone lives, DI Merton was thinking to himself.

He said, "Right, we're done here. Now we're expected, I hope, at the next call about 1400 hours. We'll call at the *George and Dragon* on the way."

"More inquiries, Sir?" asked DC Harlow.

"No. Lunch." said DI Merton.

◆ ◆ ◆

"Textbook case. Great job. Well done everybody". Sgt Harris was in euphoric mood. The team had returned to Divisional HQ from Tallows in Beech Street with boxes full of retrieved stolen silver and jewellery and three prisoners who were now downstairs in the cells.

He continued, "Special thanks to Taylor who made the connection between the two premises in the first place and you lads from Central who set the whole thing up so efficiently. There's going to be a lot of crimes on the books cleared up today. Or should be. The boss will be over the moon."

Earlier, at 1000 hours, the Tallows had been surprised by the knock on the door and by being shown the search warrant. The telephone in the house had been swiftly secured. It was not long before the stolen property was found, barely hidden, so confident were the Tallows. A radio call to the two uniformed constables in the panda had instantly secured the arrest of the young man in the 'Second Chance' shop. The two younger Tallows were indeed brothers, Mark at the scrapyard with his dad and Russell ran the shop. A further call to Traffic Division led to the impounding of the Bedford lorry which might give up some evidence.

Charges of receiving stolen property would soon be brought.

"But I guess they'll be bailed for the time being," said DS Harris, grinning. "We wouldn't want the scrap metal collection business in Millwood and district to grind to a halt, would we?"

◆ ◆ ◆

As the Rover was approaching Millwood, DI Merton said to DC Harlow, "Just before we get to the pub, We'll make a swift call on Margaret to keep in touch with her. And there's something else I want to do there. Just follow my lead. Have you got a couple of large evidence bags? Keep them under wraps until we need them. A bit of a surprise is in order, I think."

Graham Finlay answered the door. "Oh. Hello Inspector. Come in. Back so soon?" Graham could be a man of few words.

They greeted Margaret, assuring her everything was being done in the investigation, reiterating that these things take a little time but usually, once the pieces of the puzzle were put in their places, the truth of the matter would emerge.

"How are you, anyway?"

Margaret told him that, each day, she was coming to terms with what had happened, though it was very early days and things would never be the same again. She was clearly concerned about her own future but no doubt there would be help forthcoming. A social worker had made an appointment to visit tomorrow.

Graham said his boss had granted him compassionate leave this week but he must be back at work for his weekend shifts, so he and Sarah would need to return home on Friday. No doubt he would also be allowed the necessary time to attend the funeral, in due course. He had been taken to officially identify the body of his sister. That had shaken him up considerably but he was alright now.

"Good," said DI Merton. "I know it must be difficult and we are trying our very best. Now, there's just one thing I must do while I am here. When I was here with DC Taylor yesterday, there was something in Sally's room I now want to take another look at. Is it alright if we go up? Sorry to be a nuisance. We'll only be a couple of minutes."

"Help yourself, you know the way," said Graham who seemed to be getting more and more dejected. Merton thought he probably had good cause. A lot of responsibility was falling upon him, the older brother. He probably didn't know how to cope very well.

Merton and Harlow went up to Sally's bedroom. DI Merton was hoping the shoe box was still there. If it wasn't, a whole new kettle of fish would open up.

The shoe box was still there, on the hidden shelf in the wardrobe. Nothing inside had been disturbed. DC Harlow quickly glanced at the contents and put the whole thing with the lid in place in an evidence bag. The folder from the drawer in the dressing table went into the other bag. Both bags were marked and sealed and they took them downstairs.

"Now, don't be alarmed at what I'm going to tell you. It's probably nothing at all but we have to check every detail in case it's important." DI Merton was using his kindest voice. Margaret, Graham and Sarah were looking at the bags.

"This is just a formality. I'm sure everything will work out fine. But I am obliged to seize these items, which were in Sally's bedroom, as there is a suspicion they may have been involved in crime. They may also help in our investigations."

He had chosen his words carefully so as to limit the alarm caused to these people, Margaret especially. "I will give you a receipt for the items. They are a shoe box and contents which were in Sally's wardrobe and a folder containing a variety of documents which were in a drawer of her dressing table. Once the investigation is complete and if all is in order, they will be returned to you."

He quickly wrote out the receipt and gave it to Graham. He, Sarah and Margaret could do little but accept and nod their agreement. They showed no sign of concern and clearly had no idea what the significance of these things might be.

With that, Merton and Harlow, having said they would stay in touch, were gone.

In the car, Merton said, "This car's got a pretty secure boot, I'm sure, but it's not worth the risk, leaving them in a pub car park. We're taking these straight to the property room at DHQ and booking them in. Sorry but we'll have to skip the *George and Dragon* after all."

"No problem, Sir." said DC Harlow. "I've brought sandwiches. You're welcome to share them."

◆ ◆ ◆

"Have we got a tape measure knocking around the office somewhere?" DI Merton asked.

Harlow produced a tape from the back of a drawer. "I guess we're going to measure that fence, Sir?"

"Yes. Might be useful to know, for evidence but we'll need to know Sally's exact height as well. And the heels on her shoes. Why does it always get so complicated these days? It's all about the details, Harlow. Remember that. Never forget the details. I'll phone Franklyn later. Won't take a minute to call in at the car park and do it on the way to see Dylan … what's the name … Jenkins. Sounds like a Welshman."

"Boots, Sir. Sally was wearing boots," said Harlow.

At the car park they took careful measurements of the fence by the side of the footpath at several points. The average was calculated at five feet and one inch and noted in DI Merton's pocket book. He said, "Right, now for Mr. Dylan Jenkins.

Mr. Jenkins' house in Sherwood Drive, Millwood was in a small, modern estate of modest semi-detached houses with neat front gardens. Merton rang the bell and Dylan opened the door, accompanied by a lively young springer spaniel.

"Sorry we're a bit late, Mr Jenkins. I'm DI Merton. This is DC Harlow." Warrant cards were displayed.

"Come in, come in. I gather you're doing the rounds of people who knew Sally. Awful, isn't it? How are you getting on? Was it somebody mugged her? Can't really believe it."

They sat down around a table in the back room.

DI Merton said, "We won't keep you long Mr.

Jenkins. It's just that it is important that we speak with everyone who knew Sally Weston, especially those who were with her last Thursday evening."

"Weston?" said Dylan. "I don't even think I ever knew that was her other name. It was always just Sally. Oh dear. Just shows how you think you know someone, doesn't it?"

"So, we're trying to establish when each of the Thursday Club members and anyone else for that matter, left the bar of the *George and Dragon*. What about you, Sir?"

"Well, let me see," began Dylan. "It can't have been long after 9.30 because I like to get home to see News at Ten. Anna Ford, you know." He smiled. "It only takes about ten or fifteen minutes. Not quite as quick walking as I used to be. Icy it was too." Then he became serious. "None of that matters though, does it? It's Sally isn't it, we have to think about? It's funny, the last thing I did for her was buy some drinks. Poor Sally."

"I'd like you to think carefully, Mr. Jenkins, if you would please," said Merton. "When you left the bar to walk home, which door did you use?"

"Always use the side door, onto the footpath".

"You would turn left on the footpath, then right into the town square and then it's just ten or fifteen minutes' walk home?"

"That's about it." said Dylan.

"So you left just after 9.30. Did anyone leave at about the same time as you?" asked Merton.

No ... no, don't think so. Bruce was talking to Jim ... old RAF mates they are. Tom was at the bar. Norman was in his usual place by the fire ... he usually hangs on for a bit. No, nobody at the same time. But I don't think anybody stays on very long, apart from Norman of course."

DC Harlow said, "Bruce Morgan lives near you, doesn't he? Do you walk home together at all on Thursday nights?"

"Yes, quite often we do but we don't hang around waiting if one of us is talking, you know, to his RAF mates, or whatever." replied Dylan. "It's only ten minutes anyway. Sometimes see him when we're out walking the dogs. Not often. Last time was about a week ago."

DI Merton and DC Harlow stood up. "Thank you for your help, Mr. Jenkins. It really has been useful."

As they got to the door, Merton turned and said, "Mr. Jenkins, just now I think you said something about the last thing you did for Sally was to buy some drinks. What did you mean?"

"Oh, nothing much really. It was often the

same, Sally used to arrive and sit at the back of the table and said she would buy some drinks. There were usually a few of us with a nearly empty glass. She would give one of us a five pound note and we'd go to the bar for her. It was me last Thursday. That's all I meant."

"On Thursday, was there any change from the five pound note?" Merton asked.

Dylan thought for a moment. "Yes, I think so … yes … it was a pound and something. She put it back in her bag."

"What did Sally drink, Dylan?"

"Sally always drank Martinis".

"Thank you again, Sir." The detectives turned to the door.

"Hope you catch them soon. We're going to miss Sally," said Dylan.

❖ ❖ ❖

Back in the car, outside Dylan Jenkins' house, DC Harlow asked, "Will we be including Bruce Morgan in the inquiries, Sir? I know he called it in when he discovered Sally and we've got his statement covering that. But he might be able to throw some light on who left the bar when and so on. On the off-chance. And he lives just around the corner from here."

DI Merton thought for a moment. "You didn't see Bruce Morgan that morning, did you? He was in a right old state. But you've got a point, Harlow. As we're so close we might as well see if he's in. Shouldn't take a minute."

They drove around to 33 Lyndon Avenue. The door was opened by Bruce Morgan accompanied by his black Labrador dog which appeared very pleased to have visitors. Bruce said, "Oh. It's you. I didn't know when it would be. Is it about the inquest? They said I would have to attend it."

"Sorry to disturb you, Mr. Morgan," said DI Merton. "It won't take more than a few minutes. Could we come in for a moment please?"

Inside, in the hallway which wasn't very big and was made smaller by a well-laden coat stand, DI Merton was saying that it was not necessary to sit down, just for a couple of questions. He said, "Firstly, how are you now? Recovered, I hope? You had quite a nasty experience on Friday, didn't you?"

"Thanks, yes," replied Bruce in his customary slow way of speaking. "I know I made a bit of a fool of myself, didn't I? Honestly, I didn't think that was me at all. But, yes, it was a big shock. Still keeps me awake at night. No doubt it'll settle down in time. Jennifer, my wife, she's been a big help. She's out just at the moment. Does some part time at Tesco's. Checkout. Oh, sorry, I'm going on a bit. What did you want to know?"

"Well," said Merton, "We're asking all the members of the Thursday Club the same thing really. It helps us to know who was where and when and so what they might have seen. If that makes sense. When did you leave the bar of the *George and Dragon* to come home?"

Bruce thought for a moment. "Well … oh dear … my memory these days … it was … well, my usual time. I think most of them had gone. I was talking to Jim about the team for next week's match. Only a few minutes. Tom was there and Norman of course. Dylan had gone, I think. Sometimes we walk back together. He's only just around the corner from here."

"Which door from the bar did you use? Did you see anyone as you left?"

"The side door. On to the footpath. No. Dylan had gone as I said. Didn't see anybody else. On the way back there were one or two people in the Square. Not many. Too cold to be out. I was glad to get back home. Sorry, I'm not much use am I?"

"That's fine, Mr. Morgan, said Merton. "Everything is helpful. The process of elimination you see. You'll hear about the inquest, I'm sure. Not too long now, I should think, depending on the Coroner. We had better get going. Thanks again, very much, for your help last week."

By now it was dark. On the drive back to the office, DI Merton said, "Well, we've talked to everybody likely to be in the frame. We'll get together in the morning and put our thinking caps on."

"Yes, Sir," said DC Harlow.

CHAPTER 15

"Good morning everybody". DI Merton had cleared his throat and was summing up the situation. "It's Wednesday. Five days into the case, so we'll get straight to business. We've got a lot of facts together. Most of those facts are true but there's bound to be a few that are suspect. Let's now talk it all through and see if we can make sense of Sally Weston's murder. This morning, nobody's idea will be wrong or stupid. As an example of what I mean I will kick off the discussion with what you're all going to think is really stupid." He paused for at least ten seconds while the team waited.

"Does anybody know anything about the moon?" he asked.

The team had gathered first thing that morning. Some were still congratulating themselves on yesterday's success and were now planning a strategy to go and collar a minor local gang of thieves who had used Tallows as their receivers. DCs Firth and Oldroyd were planning a big surprise for the gang. But not just yet. They had received information the thieves they wanted used a particular pub in Lupton town centre at lunchtimes and it would be a good place to pick them up. That was for later this morning.

For the time being, they were joining in the discussion about the current state of the murder investigation.

"Are there any budding astronomers here? Anyone know anything about the moon?" Merton repeated.

DC Firth was still a bit fired up with the good result but said, "It used to be my hobby. Astronomy. The moon, Sir? Basically it behaves a bit like the sun. Rises roughly north-east to east and sets in the west but might be a bit further north, I think. Rises at all different times as well, depending on the season and so on, which makes things awkward. And of course it has phases, like it was full moon last Thursday. An American flag was planted on it nine years ago. Sorry, Sir."

Ignoring the quip, Merton said, "Okay, roughly where would our full moon have been in the sky last Thursday at 2130 hours?

Almost wishing he hadn't spoken up, DC Firth

said, "Well, I can't be completely sure. It could be looked up. So I'm guessing around east or thereabouts. Give or take. Maybe a bit further round. Depends what time moon rise was."

"Alright," Merton said. "We'll work on that basis for the moment. Roughly east it is." He went over and examined the map which Taylor had placed on the pin board. "This street plan is fairly large scale of Millwood and some surroundings. Big enough anyway to pick out some significant buildings. The *George and Dragon* is a significant building obviously and it's clearly shown. It faces roughly south. Agreed? So, if the moon was here in the east or even a bit further round, the building would throw a shadow onto the footpath next to it. On its western side. Am I right?"

There was general assent from those trying to keep up. DC Harlow said, "And the moon throws very dark shadows because there's not much light to bounce back into them, like the sun does when it's out in the daytime."

"Yes, good point, Harlow. Even better. So, if somebody was standing in that shadow, on the footpath next to the wall of the pub, they would be almost invisible to anyone coming out of the bar door and turning left towards the Square. I take it we can all agree on that?"

All this talk about the moon was taking everyone by surprise. DI Merton sensed that was the case. He said, "Well, you're probably thinking the old man's losing his marbles. But we've got to start somewhere, haven't we? So far, every member of the Thursday Club has told us what they were doing that night, what time they left and so on. Each one of them has given us an innocent and plausible account."

"Okay, pay attention. Fred left first and walked home. But he could have waited for Sally, unseen in that shadow."

"He's quite an old chap isn't he? Could he have done it?" DC Harlow said.

"We're just going through them all for the moment. We can all think about each one. Anyone can chip in, no matter how stupid it seems, as I said before. Stupid is probably what we need right now."

"The Lowesbys went out of the car park door from the hallway and they must have scraped the ice from their windscreen although they didn't mention doing that. They say they didn't see anyone. Rob Jordan says that he said goodnight to them."

"In fact, Rob Jordan was next out of the back door into the car park. He passed the Lowesbys and also noticed Jim's red MG with a blanket across the windscreen. He went to his car parked by the fence next to the footpath and started scraping the ice from his windscreen. That took him about ten minutes, he said. Hard frost, likes to do a thorough job. I can believe that; he was a mechanic on Spitfires in the War. What happened next, Harlow?"

"Oh, right," began Harlow, "During that ten minutes of scraping, with his back to the fence, he was aware, just out of the corner of his eye, of a couple walking down the footpath. Never thought anything of it. Locals, he thought, going home from the pub. Rob's not local and doesn't know the footpath goes nowhere really. Oh, yes, he was aware one was taller than the other. We measured the fence at five feet one inch. He's given a statement."

DI Merton said, "With all that scraping going on in the car park, I can't see Rob Jordan or the Lowesbys on our shortlist. But Rob's evidence seems useful. Everybody agree?"

Taylor hadn't spoken so far. She was still glowing from her success and accolades yesterday and now wanted to add more kudos to her reputation. Cautiously, she said, "From what I have gathered so far, it seems any offer by any of the men to gallantly walk Sally home, even though none of them knew where she lived, was always declined by Sally. So ... I gather she left the bar next ... on her own. I think that was from the side door. Do you think she might have waited in the moon shadow by the pub wall for someone?"

"That would have to be someone she knew," said Harris. "It would have to be a Thursday Club member, surely? If it's somebody else altogether, we're up a gum tree."

"While we are scrambling around up gum trees," intervened Merton, "is there, realistically, anyone else in the frame? Sally's brother, Graham, after her loot? Oh, yes, I'll come to that in a minute. Where she worked? That pompous so-and-so, Armstrong or any of the workers in the factory? Can't see it but if we wanted to look at that it would take forever." Merton paused.

"Excuse me, Sir, said DC Oldroyd, there's the drug-taking folk in the wood. They weren't there last night. I didn't think they would be somehow. All the activity has sent them packing. We'll try again tomorrow night."

"Look," said Merton, "I shouldn't bother with tomorrow night. I agree with you. All through this I've never thought Sally had anything to do with them or any other random mugger who happened to be waiting for her. I just can't see how that would fit."

"Right, thank you, Sir, said DC Oldroyd. We'll have to be off now. We've got that appointment at the *Crown* in Lupton to get sorted out for." He and DC Firth grinned. "See you later." They left.

"Alright," said Merton, "Is there anyone else any of you think should be put in the frame? If not, we'll return to talking about the Thursday Club. Yes, Taylor, you are right. Sally seems to have been the next to leave and may well have waited in that shadow. Otherwise she would have walked straight home. Which in turn means she was waiting for someone. Find that someone and we've got him. We'll have to look each one of them in the eye and ask them."

"After Sally left the bar there were five of them left," said DC Harlow. "I think Bruce left after Sally. Could that be significant? No, sorry, Dylan was first. He didn't wait for Bruce as he sometimes does. Then it was Bruce. Jim and Tom went in Jim's car which seems to rule them out although Jim could have dropped Tom off and come back. It's not that far. Norman was a long way behind the others but I suppose he could have gone out and come back and finished his pint without anyone noticing. Sorry to go on, Sir."

"That's okay," said Merton, "you've summed it up well, Harlow. So well, in fact, that we now have that complete list of Thursday Club members in the order they left the bar of the *George and Dragon* that night. You'll notice that Sally herself is roughly in the middle of the order of leaving.

"Now, Rob Jordan gave us some vital information yesterday. For the moment we've got to assume that the couple he saw out of the corner of his eye included Sally and one other. Why would any other couple be walking in that direction, towards the wood, at the crucial time? Sally died between 2100 and midnight."

"One was taller than the other," said Taylor. "Are all the men taller than Sally? ... than Sally was?"

Everyone thought about it and were in agreement that was the case, although Dylan Jenkins would only be taller by an inch or so.

Taylor continued, "We seem to have ruled out the guys who left before her, Don't we? Fred, Raymond and Rob. Is that right?"

"I'm pretty sure that's right," said Merton, sounding a bit impatient. "Before we go speculating any further, lets cover something we haven't really thought about much. It's actually pretty vital. That is, why was she killed? Motive. Motive. Motive. That vital but often elusive piece of the jigsaw. Any ideas yet?

"We were discussing it the other night, weren't we, Sir?" Sergeant Harris said. "You were considering blackmail."

Between them, Merton and Harris related what Jim Wheatland had told them on Monday evening.

"Jim Wheatland is a rich man because we all drink his beer." said Merton. "So he doesn't mind contributing financially to help Sally and Margaret out. The sums increased over the years until lately it amounted to a substantial regular amount, £50 a month. They both seemed very happy about it but I'm guessing that Sally knew she was on to a good thing and wasn't going to let it go. You can call it what you like. Sergeant Harris calls it prostitution. But they are two consenting adults, well known to each other, so I prefer blackmail. A judge probably wouldn't agree to either. However ..." Merton paused.

"In any case," Harris said, "why would Jim kill his blackmailer? The sums involved were petty cash to him and presumably they would go on enjoying each other's company. Unless there's something he hasn't told us."

"More to the point at the moment," said Merton, "Harris and Taylor were out enjoying themselves yesterday, collaring thieving scrap merchants. While that was going on, Harlow and I were seizing what I think could be argued to be the proceeds of real crime. Taylor had seen it on our first visit to Sally's bedroom and she was worried that a shoe box full of thousands of pounds might suddenly disappear, even though it was fairly well hidden. But at that time I couldn't link it to a crime. Yesterday, though, I had seen the possibility of blackmail and so could justify seizure on suspicion that it might be the proceeds of crime. How much was there, Harlow?"

"When I booked it in, the cash was counted. Adding that to the Post Office account it came to just over eleven grand," said Harlow. "We've also got the documents from the drawer which could have been used as the threat."

"So, Sally had around eleven grand stashed away," said Merton. "If I'm correct, Jim Wheatland's contributions over the eight years they'd been going out together didn't amount to anywhere near a quarter of that. Especially after Sally had used what was necessary to add to her wages to support her and Margaret."

That conclusion took a few moments to sink in. Then Taylor said, "So Sally was a blackmailer. How else would she have got that money? She was being paid a pittance at Armstrong's. So, there must have been someone else she was blackmailing? One of the Thursday Club people or somebody else we don't know about?"

"I'm going to suggest a scenario for us all to think about," said DI Merton. "Then we can think about it while we have a break, a breath of fresh air or whatever you want to do. "

"It's very simple. In Sally's diary, every first Thursday of the month is circled. She meets up with someone outside the pub and they go for a short walk together, a bit secluded. The wood, let's say. Last Thursday anyway. The cash gets handed over and then she continues on the shortcut to Beech Street and home. Better in the Summer, I admit. But by last Thursday, whoever was being blackmailed had decided he'd had enough. And wham. No more Sally. Bear in mind she only had a pound in her handbag. No money had been handed over to her first."

After a pause to allow that to sink in, Merton said, "One final thing to bear in mind. We know that about ten years ago, a few years after the car crash, Sally gave birth. The baby was named Timothy. He was adopted three months later. She never revealed to anyone who the father was. We have the papers from Sally's drawer documenting those events. No mention of the father on the birth certificate. I think that's a copy. I'll leave you with those thoughts."

◆ ◆ ◆

The detectives consumed their sandwiches and mugs of tea almost silently as they forced their minds to try to think of the one missing detail which would unlock the mystery.

The first of them to speak as they re-assembled was Taylor. "Sir, if there was a regular pattern of Sally and her victim meeting up for a walk along the footpath to the wood every first Thursday and this had gone on for many years, wouldn't someone have noticed it? Even now they would be putting two and two together."

"There will always be flaws in such ideas, Taylor. I agree with you," said Merton. "But, if you think about it, last Thursday was unusual. Rob Jordan was delayed by ten minutes while he cleared his windscreen and even then only caught a glimpse of an anonymous couple on the footpath out of the corner of his eye. We're only talking about once a month, I think, because of the diary. And they would take care to be unobserved, I imagine. There's an outside chance Rob Jordan lied to us to protect a friend, or himself even. But I doubt that. You were there, Harlow. Do you agree?"

DC Harlow's reply was an emphatic, "Yes, Sir." He went on, "It must surely be one of those who left after Sally. Dylan or Bruce. Well, no, not Bruce, I guess. Jim, but only if he came back after dropping Tom off. Or Norman who might have slipped out of the bar unnoticed."

As it sometimes happens in the CID office, today there was the unmistakeable feeling that they were going around in circles.

There was a long pause. DS Harris, untypically, appeared to be undecided if he should speak, "Sir, this will probably end up in the 'stupid' category, I know, but it's been a bit of a niggle all the time. I've just been thinking it through again."

"Let's hear it, Sergeant," Merton said.

"Well, you know when we first arrived on scene last Friday - you, Taylor and me - that was when we first met Bruce Morgan. He was in a state of shock which was understandable. The sergeant from the area car said they had found him in a collapsed state, on his knees in the phone box with his arms around his dog. One glove was on the floor."

"Go on, Harris," encouraged DI Merton.

"Well, the first thing is, when Bruce Morgan dialled three nines it must have happened a good fifteen minutes, I should think, after he had discovered Sally's body. Maybe more. He made the call. Control sent a response and they passed the message through to us here at the office. We were pretty quick off the mark but it's about six miles. I guess we arrived in Beech Street around half an hour later. Uniform had walked Morgan down Beech Street and into the wood where he had pointed out where the body was. He was brought back to the street and they sat him in the back of the panda. We got there soon after. Then you spoke to him and I was next to you. Even then, he seemed to be in considerable shock. I remember him clearly. He was mumbling about walking the dog and trying to say something that sounded like "but ... but ... but ..." and he was trying to get hold of your arm. As I say, a right state."

Taylor was listening intently, believing she might have an understanding of what DS Harris was leading up to.

DI Merton asked him where this was going.

"Well, Sir, I said this might all be in the stupid category. It's just that I have never seen anyone, in any similar circumstances, become so deeply shocked as that, not for so long anyway. He had become better later in the afternoon when I went to take his statement but he didn't seem completely right. Sort of vacant, speech still sort of wobbly, as though he wasn't really there. Just slumped in his chair.

"All I'm saying, Sir, is that here we have an ex-RAF sergeant, served throughout the War. He joined the Ambulance Service for the rest of his working days - they're both uniformed and disciplined services. He must be very used to seeing and dealing with dead bodies. Could it all have been a kind of weird act? It's just that I thought it worth mentioning."

DI Merton was thoughtful. Taylor was trying to recall the scene. DC Harlow was interested to see how the Inspector would react.

Nobody said anything while DS Harris's words sank in.

DI Merton spoke slowly, "Are you suggesting, Harris, that Bruce Morgan murdered Sally the night before and then, the following morning, he calmly walked his dog to that phone box and began to put on that act. An over the top act of appearing shocked - which he kept going for most of the rest of the day? All to put himself in the clear?"

"Not quite." Harris said, losing a bit of confidence. "Well, I suppose that's one possibility. I just don't know. Which is why it's been niggling all this time."

After a pause, Harris continued. "My way of thinking of it is that he's actually quite genuine. He's not putting on an act. Yes, let's say he murdered Sally. Perhaps it's him she was blackmailing. But there's something about Bruce Morgan. As I said, he seems a bit vague and distant. Slow. It would need a psychiatrist to sort it out. But I think I've read somewhere that there's some mental syndrome or other that says that you can do a terrible thing and then your brain automatically blots it out. So what happened on Friday morning could have been all quite genuine. But somewhere in his mind it was still there and compounded the shocked reaction."

DS Harris sat back in his chair and spread his arms in a kind of take it or leave it gesture. "For what it's worth, Sir," he said.

Again, nobody spoke for a while.

"I was there that morning," ventured Taylor. "He was certainly in a state. I think it was genuine. You couldn't put on an act like that and keep it up for two or three hours convincingly."

DI Merton stood up and began to pace around the office. Harris had clearly given him something to think about.

Abruptly, he said, "Anyone got any other suggestions?" They hadn't.

"Well then, Mr. Bruce Morgan it is then. We've got to dig deep, haven't we? No good thinking we could knock on his door and ask him to confess on the basis that he's a good actor. We can't get him to lie down on a psychiatrist's couch and wait for him to tell his life story which happens to include murder, can we?"

He paused and said, "We need something else. I've got an idea. I've only done it once before and it was useful then. Force control keeps a recording of three nines calls. Would it be useful to hear what Bruce Morgan actually said, in his shocked state?"

There was a vigorous nodding. "Right, someone find me the incident number. It should be on the first message, the first document in the main file, if you've been keeping on top of the paperwork that is."

Merton picked up a small booklet, the 'Force Internal Telephone Directory'. He dialled the four digit direct line number of the Force Control Inspector.

The call was promptly answered, "Control Room, Inspector Leeman."

"Frank! You're still on afternoons then. It's John Merton."

"Hello, mate. I wasn't expecting to be. We quite often swap duties around to help each other out. Not like you though ... you can skive off when you like," Frank Leeman teased."

"We work when we can catch the criminals. Not when there's a desk to drive." Merton returned the banter. "Now look, Frank. You record the three nines calls, I seem to remember?"

"We record all calls coming through here," Frank said. "What do you need?"

"It's the call for the murder case I'm on ..." Taylor held out the message document. "... Here it is ... incident 84 of 781107."

"Okay. The technical lads just down the corridor can find it for you. I'll let them know. When will you come in?"

"We'll be on our way any minute now," replied Merton. "Is that okay?"

"Sure. Twenty-four hours a day service here John," said Leeman. Merton laughed and put down the phone.

"Right, Sergeant Harris, We'll go and find out if Bruce Morgan can tell us anything more. I'm sure you two have a great deal of report writing and filing to do and … oh yes, I imagine you'll be able to help DCs Firth and Oldroyd celebrate nabbing a few real criminals. They ought to be back soon. Probably downstairs in custody as we speak."

"Grab your coat, Sergeant."

◆ ◆ ◆

The drive in the Rover to Headquarters was mainly in silence. At one point, DS Harris said, "Do you really think there could be something in this, Sir? I'm not really sure."

"Always have an open mind. Investigate everything that comes up, especially if you've got nothing else. Something like Sherlock Holmes said to Doctor Watson, I seem to remember. I think there's a posh name for it these days." Merton replied.

"Of course," he went on, "if this does come to nothing, we'll have a lot of digging around the other Thursday Club members to do. At the moment we're just going on what they've told us so far. For example, Robert Jordan was very convincing. He gave us valuable information. We think. We got his signed statement. But even he could have been lying through his teeth about scraping his car windscreen and all that. He was in the right place. Perhaps it was him."

After another pause, Merton smiled to himself, feeling a bit of confidence rising. He continued mischievously, "Of course it could be like *The Orient Express*, couldn't it, Harris?"

"The what express, Sir?"

"You know. Agatha Christie. Hercule Poirot. I think they've even made a film of it. *Murder on the Orient Express.* We're fortunate, we've only got about nine suspects. Poirot had a dozen. Now, that murder mystery had an interesting ending, didn't it?"

"Did it?" Harris said. "But I don't think I've read it. Or seen it. What happened, Sir?"

"If you've not read it, Harris, I'm not going to spoil it for you.," Merton chuckled to himself.

They drove through the wide gates and up the drive to Force Headquarters.

◆ ◆ ◆

"Didn't think I'd see you again quite so soon." Inspector Leeman had met them at the Control Room door and DS Harris was introduced.

"I did a stint in here once, Sir," said Harris. "Just a couple of months experience when I was on probation. It's been re-fitted since. Very plush. Back then it was a map on a table with some wooden blocks we moved around to show where the mobiles were and a few desks with old fashioned telephones."

"You're wanting the latest in technology today though, aren't you?" said Frank Leeman. "Voice recording no less. Hope it helps. I'll take you through."

A door at the far end of the long room led to a corridor with several doors. One said "Fingerprint Bureau".

"Never heard of most of these departments," said Merton as they walked past some of the labels on the doors. They came to a door marked 'Comms Technical'. After knocking they went in to be greeted by two young men. Everywhere there were benches with screens, wires, aerials, humming test equipment.

"Hello, I'm Ian, this is Neil. Welcome to the department which keeps the Force running," Ian smiled, slipping into a practised introductory speech to impress occasional visitors. "Basically the Force and Divisional radio systems and the internal telephone system. Oh, and all the gear in the control rooms and the mobiles. On call 24 hours a day. At your service." He seemed to enjoy having visitors to observe what they did in their back room.

"You want to hear a recording from a three nines call? Since Inspector Leeman asked us, we've pinned it down and made a secondary tape you can listen to."

Inspector Leeman said, "I'd better get back to the coal face. I'll leave you to the tender mercies of these guys. They know their stuff. Hope you find what you need. Cheerio, John. See you sometime."

DI Merton and DS Harris turned to a tape machine on the bench in front of them.

"Ready?" Ian asked. They nodded and Ian pressed a button. Surprisingly clearly, an automated metallic female voice stated, "Friday ... seven ... November ... ten ... forty-four". There was a pause and a click and then the voice of the Control Room operator.

"Police, can I help you?"

There was the distinct sound of fast heavy breathing.

"Can I help you? Take your time. What's happened?"

"There's a dead body ... In the wood." The male, croaking voice was clearly very stressed.

"Okay, Sir, which wood?"

"I'm sure she's dead ... not moving." The laboured breathing continued.

"What's your name?"

Very faintly, within the background hum of the Control Room, another voice had asked, "Where?"

"I ..." The voice was instantly drowned out by a tremendously loud, high-pitched noise lasting just 5 or 6 seconds. It came so suddenly that Merton and Harris instinctively moved back from the machine.

"What was that?" the operator had asked. The faint sound of sobbing could be heard for a few seconds.

"It was the jet planes flying over. Training," the voice had recovered a little.

"That's okay then, Sir. Would you tell me where you are please?"

"I ... I'm in the phone box. Forest Road. It's in the woods off Beech Street," and after a pause, "Millwood."

"Listen, Sir, I didn't get your name," the Control Room operator had said.

"Morgan. Bruce Morgan."

"Where do you live?"

There was a sigh. "33 Lyndon Avenue."

"Please stay where you are, Sir. Help is on the way."

There were no more voices but for a few more seconds there were sounds, firstly as if the telephone receiver had been dropped, then what sounded like an animal whining.

There was a click and the automated voice returned, "Ends ... ten ... forty-seven".

"Poor guy", said Ian. 'sounds in a bit of a bad way... Oh, yes, you can take this tape with you if it helps. We can even make other copies if you need them or for evidential purposes. We sometimes get requests for that."

DI Merton said nothing for a moment, then, "Would you play it again please?"

"Sure," said Ian, rewinding the tape and then playing it. Both detectives leaned forward, listening intently.

When it was done, Harris said, "You're thinking what I'm thinking, aren't you, Sir? Bruce was saying something just as the planes went over. It was 'I' something but it got drowned out."

"That's right," said Merton. "He'd just been asked to say where he was and after the noise drowned him out, just a bit further on he says, 'I'm in the phone box'. That was probably it."

"If it's of any help gents," said Ian, "I might be able to let you hear him speak over the noise. It's all a matter of sound frequencies, you see. The noise of a screaming jet plane will probably be quite a high frequency. I think so. Higher than a man's voice, for sure. I could have a go at separating the two if you like. It's a bit basic and Heath Robinson but it might work. No guarantees. Shall I try?"

"Good of you, Ian," said Merton. "Yes please."

"Right, let's plug that into that and bring that over here. Rewind. Twiddle a few knobs. Switch the oscilloscope on. It might take a few goes. It's just that bit in the middle you want, isn't it, with the jet noise? If it works we can do you tapes with the revised content. Here goes."

At the first attempt they could just about detect that there might be a voice over the jet sound which had faded a little. Ian tried twice more, reducing the amount of the jet noise while leaving the voice clearer but just not quite clear enough.

"I think we're getting closer. One more go might do it," said Harris.

At the fourth attempt, the high pitched noise of the jet had receded just sufficiently. Bruce Morgan's still faint voice could be heard just distinctly enough.

"I killed her, I killed her," his voice sobbed.

◆ ◆ ◆

They arrived back at the West Division CID office much later than they had anticipated. All that technical stuff had taken time.

The others were waiting for them, unwilling to leave before knowing if anything had come of listening to Bruce Morgan's three nines call.

The four DCs, Taylor, Harlow, Firth and Oldroyd were all in a good mood anyway. The jewellery and silver burglary gang had been nicked by Firth and Oldroyd. The three targets had been, as expected, enjoying their liquid lunches in the bar of the *Crown* in Lupton town centre. With uniform backup it had been an easy collar and they were now residing downstairs in the cells awaiting their appearance in the Magistrate's Court tomorrow morning.

"Aren't we doing well?" DI Merton appeared to be in a good mood. "What with DC Harlow's rugby tackle the other day closing down a good few car crime cases. How is your elbow coming along by the way?"

"Almost as good as new, thank you, Sir." grinned Harlow.

"Then Taylor spots the jewellery and silver receivers because they'd painted two signs using the same yellow pot of paint. Well done, Taylor. In fact, Taylor, from now on we'll call you DC Taylor. Consider it promotion of sorts. And we'd better find you your own desk. Welcome to the team DC Taylor."

"Thank you, Sir," said DC Taylor with a wide smile.

"And all of that led to Firth and Oldroyd being able to nab the jewellery gang today. Well done lads. I reckon you'll be able to get back to Central Division by the end of the week."

Everyone laughed but really they were all patiently anticipating the news which Merton and Harris might have brought, especially as Sergeant Harris hadn't stopped grinning since he had walked through the door. Merton was clearly spinning out the agony.

DI Merton said, "Yes, our news appears to be good too." He brought out of his briefcase a portable cassette tape recorder and two cassettes. "I borrowed this from the technical people at HQ because I couldn't remember if we had one here. Plug it in someone."

He inserted the cassette marked 'original'.

Everyone was silent as they listened.

"So," said Merton, "we know Bruce Morgan was very upset, in shock or whatever you want to call it. And they got enough out of him to be able to send a prompt response. We sort of know the rest. But do we? The noise of those jets going over drowned out something he was saying, didn't it? Well, after we'd listened to it a couple of times, Ian, the technical chap at HQ, chipped in and asked if we wanted the noise of the jets removing. Something to do with difference in noise frequencies. Of course we did, we told him. He did some wizardry with his electronic gear and produced this."

The second cassette tape was played and everyone heard Bruce Morgan say, "I killed her, I killed her".

There was silence for a moment and then Sergeant Harris simply said, "If those jets hadn't gone over at that precise moment, Control Room would have picked up those words and Morgan would have been arrested on the spot. Job done last Friday. Well, almost."

"As far as Morgan was concerned, he had confessed on the phone," said DC Taylor. "He was expecting to be arrested, I suppose. Why didn't he tell us or the area car crew when we got to him?"

"Maybe he was trying to," said DS Harris, "Remember, we were saying this morning that when you were talking to him in the panda, Sir, he was trying to say something but couldn't get it out. He was trying to clutch your arm as well. But because he appeared to be in such a state of shock the words wouldn't come out."

"Then, perhaps after he had been taken home, he realised that, because he hadn't been arrested there and then, he might have got away with it and decided to keep quiet." DC Harlow offered. "I wasn't there on Friday but when we were talking to him yesterday he didn't seem quite right. Not quite with it. I couldn't really put my finger on it. Perhaps we now know why."

"Okay, okay, okay." DI Merton brought the speculation to a halt. "I can't imagine that Bruce Morgan will suddenly do a runner, can you? So I'm not going to go and arrest him today. Let him have one more night with his wife and dog. I suspect he won't get any more."

He went on, "I believe Morgan is basically a decent chap. Something happened to make him snap. We don't know what it was yet. Not really. If Sally was not blackmailing him though, as we were talking about earlier because of Jim Wheatland, I really don't know what it could be. Everybody loved Sally."

"If it is blackmail, we need to know about his finances. So, Sergeant Harris, first chance in the morning, I want you to go to that bank in Millwood town square. I'm guessing he probably banks there. Get his statements for the last few years. We'll have a look at them. It might help."

"I wonder if he still takes his dog a walk through that wood. Or if he goes at all. Anyway, wherever he goes, let's say the walk takes an hour or so. He probably leaves home around 0900, I'm guessing, so we will knock on his door well before that tomorrow."

"Right," DI Merton concluded. "See you here as usual in the morning."

CHAPTER 16

Sergeant Harris did enjoy his lie in on Thursday morning. It wasn't worth getting to the bank in Millwood until it opened. He reckoned that might be 1000 hours.

Similarly, DCs Oldroyd and Firth were in no rush. They were due at Lupton Magistrate's Court to see the first stage of justice done to their jewellery gang. They were hoping for a remand in custody pending a trial later.

For the others, the day had started much earlier. In the CID office, DI Merton was talking to Taylor and Harlow. "You know, I think the man must be living a nightmare. He wanted to confess, he thought he had confessed on the phone but then saw a way of getting away with it. But ever since and for always, for the rest of his life, he will be living with that nightmare. He must surely have realised that. When we arrest him in an hour or so it will probably come as a big relief.

We'll see."

"His wife will be left behind I suppose," said DC Taylor.

"Thought of that," Merton said. "We don't need to be mob handed but I'll arrange for a panda to be around. We'll use a pool car. Of course, Jennifer might know what he's done anyway but somehow I doubt it. If it proves necessary, I'd like you and the panda man to stay with Jennifer for a bit. See if there's any way you can lend a hand. Contact family, that kind of thing. Aren't I good?"

"Yes, Sir." DC Taylor said.

Even for a detective with DI Merton's experience, it wasn't every working day that you arrested someone for murder. There was always something of a buzz in the office on such occasions.

"Time to go, I think," he said.

◆ ◆ ◆

Joe was padding up and down the hallway at 33 Lyndon Avenue, knowing it must be close to the time for his daily walk. For the last few days, Joe had been wondering why he wasn't getting such a good walk. He always enjoyed sniffing amongst the trees and the brambles in that wooded bit. Now it had become just two steady plods around that muddy, scrubby wasteland and then his lead was put on again to go back down the hard pavement into the busy town just to get a newspaper. Not a proper walk at all.

"Good boy. Won't be a minute," Jennifer was saying to him, as. Looking at her husband, as usual she said, "Are you okay? Feeling up to it? It's still quite cold so make sure you're well wrapped up. Here's Joe's lead. Don't forget to take some change, to pick up your newspaper, will you?"

Bruce put on his usual winter anorak and scarf and his woolly hat. "No, I won't forget this time," he said. He had decided not to tell Jennifer that he didn't walk through the wood any more. Although he thought he probably would return to doing that one day soon.

The doorbell rang. Jennifer opened the door. Police, obviously. There were three of them this time.

With warrant card in hand DI Merton said, "Hello Mrs. Morgan. We'd like to speak to Mr. Morgan again please."

Bruce heard them and came to the door, "Oh, hello, you were here before, weren't you? About Sally? Come in."

They went into the now crowded hallway. DC Taylor stood next to Jennifer.

DI Merton said, "Bruce Morgan, I am arresting you on suspicion of the murder of Sally Weston last Thursday, 6th November. You do not have to say anything unless you wish to do so but what you say may be given in evidence. Do you understand?"

Bruce's jaw dropped. "No ... no ... you don't understand ... it wasn't ... mistake ... Sally ... No ..." He stopped abruptly.

DI Merton pointed to the green anorak jacket Bruce was wearing and said, "Is this jacket the one you normally wear this time of the year?" Bruce nodded. "Did you wear it to the Thursday Club last week?" Bruce nodded again.

"We'll take it from you please". Bruce complied. The jacket was placed in an evidence bag and Bruce put on another jacket.

DC Harlow stepped up to Bruce, holding a pair of handcuffs. "Your hands please".

Bruce raised his right arm. DC Harlow lifted his left arm and snapped the handcuffs on. There was no resistance. The sight of that happening caused Jennifer to rush into the sitting room. She sat down and began to weep. DC Taylor followed her.

As they went out to the car, Merton signalled to the constable in the panda parked a few doors away. He drove it forwards.

He explained to the constable - it was PC O'Brien - that he should assist DC Taylor as required and ultimately return her to Divisional HQ.

From that moment, during the six mile drive, arriving at Divisional HQ, being processed and placed in an interview room, Bruce Morgan's head hung heavily on his shoulders and he said nothing. He sat at the table. A constable stood by the door.

Twenty minutes or so had gone by. DI Merton and DC Harlow came in to the room and took their seats. Merton asked Bruce if he wanted his solicitor present. Bruce shook his head.

"It's just a mistake. I didn't do anything to Sally," he said. He still gave the appearance of being bewildered by what was happening but, in his mind, was certain he could explain the mistake.

DI Merton decided to go straight for it rather than beat around the bush. He said, "But you told us you killed her. You said it twice when you made the 999 call. 'I've killed her, I've killed her', you said. We've listened to the recording of what you said."

Merton pulled the portable tape machine from his brief case, placed it on the table and pressed the button to play the modified recording.

"So, that's you isn't it, Mr. Morgan? You phoned the police to report you had found her body and said you had killed Sally Weston. What is there to deny? That's your confession, isn't it?"

Bruce was feeling confused, not fully understanding what was happening but knew he had got to explain it somehow. He was trying to force his head to think straight. He spoke slowly, as though trying to force the words out.

"But it wasn't like that," he said, tears welling up in his eyes again. "I gave her the money and then she went down the footpath. She always did that. No, sorry, I went part of the way with her. I always tried to tell her not to go that way but she always said it was the quickest way." He paused, trying to compose himself. "So it was my fault. I should have tried harder to stop her going that way. I always tried, despite everything. I never wanted her to come to any harm. She always refused. She wouldn't let me take her home or anything."

There was a loud knock on the interview room door.

"Not now," yelled Merton.

The knock was repeated. Merton got up and opened the door.

A constable said, "Sorry, Sir. It's a message. Urgent. And DS Harris is here, Sir."

"We'll be back in a minute. Come on, Harlow. Let's see what's urgent." Merton glanced at the constable and he and Harlow left the interview room.

◆ ◆ ◆

Earlier, as the two detectives had escorted the handcuffed Bruce Morgan out of his house and into the pool car, PC O'Brien nodded his understanding to the Inspector and, removing his cap, went into the house. DC Taylor was sitting next to Jennifer who was silently crying into her arms, resting on the table. Some time went by in silence, allowing Jennifer to try to come to terms with the shock of what had just happened.

Eventually, PC O'Brien, recognising the situation, said, "Mrs. Morgan. Do you remember me? We met last week. I came with Sergeant Harris to see you and your husband."

Jennifer lifted her head and nodded. Her face was heavily streaked with tears. "It can't have been him," she sobbed, "it just can't."

"Shall we get a cup of tea or something and then have a talk about it?" said DC Taylor, knowing full well that she was talking to the wife of a man who had confessed to murder. It was a bit overwhelming even for her and she wasn't quite sure what there was to talk about.

Jennifer nodded. PC O'Brien took the hint and busied himself with making tea in the kitchen. At the same time he was trying to placate Joe who was clearly seeking some explanations and wanting to know why he wasn't going for a walk yet. "It's alright, boy," O'Brien was saying.

There was another silence for quite a long while. Jennifer went to the bathroom to wash her face. After a while, PC O'Brien brought the teas in. "I managed to find everything," he said. "Sugar? Might be a good idea today." He was an experienced police officer and knew about such things.

They sipped tea for a while.

Jennifer said, "I really don't understand. Bruce could never do such a thing … I don't know how he will cope. He's not very well. He's not recovered properly yet. He seems alright most of the time but he has off days. He'll get better. He won't manage. He's quite forgetful." There was a short pause. "Last Thursday, wasn't it? Really cold night. I was worried about him but he was okay. He was a bit later than he sometimes is on his club nights but he was in time for us to sit and watch the News. He likes that new newsreader woman. Anna Ford, isn't it?"

Something about all of this was making DC Taylor take notice. Not recovered properly yet ...

arriving home more or less as usual? Could Jennifer be trying to cover for him, maybe? That didn't seem very likely. She looked at PC O'Brien for inspiration but he knew very little about the case and so wouldn't be much help. She was on her own.

No, something wasn't quite right. Gently, she said, "Why, what's the matter with Bruce?"

"It was his stroke that started it all. Nearly a year ago. Just before Christmas. It wasn't too bad, they said. But it's left him very weak. He can walk quite well now. A bit slow. He enjoys taking Joe for his walks. The exercise is good for him. He says he's getting better at throwing darts with his right arm. Still a bit weak though. He doesn't play in important matches yet. It's a good thing he's not left handed. I have to do most of the gardening and things like that. It affected his memory a bit as well, they said. Something about dementia. It's not too bad but he easily gets upset."

As Jennifer was speaking, DC Taylor felt a tingling icy chill pass through her body. This was completely new territory for her but she knew something was really wrong. She was thinking fast. Of course, Jennifer didn't know how Sally had been killed. She didn't know the killer must have been a strong man. Why would she? Taylor tried to recall exactly how DC Harlow, in the office, had related in some florid detail the experience of his first post mortem. She remembered what he had told them the pathologist had said. 'It must have been a man. A strong man to make a dent in Sally's skull like that'.

Well she, DC Taylor, had seen that so called dent. As a new and inexperienced detective, she was unsure of herself and instantly felt a great weight of responsibility. She must get this right and couldn't just do nothing. She wasn't sure how the procedure went in such cases or how quickly the charges against Bruce Morgan would be brought.

No, she decided, she could not do nothing. "May I use your phone, Jennifer?" Jennifer nodded.

The phone was in the hall. She dialled the number of the front desk at Divisional HQ and spoke quietly. "Sarge, It's DC Taylor. I need to speak to DI Merton urgently."

"He's conducting an interview at the moment, DC Taylor."

"I know, it's about that interview," she said determinedly, "It's very important information. I need to speak to him now. I will hold while you get him."

Merton came to the phone a few minutes

later. Taylor related what she had just been told.

After a thoughtful silence, Merton said, "That does make a difference, doesn't it?" Another silence. "Just hold the fort for a while. Give me the phone number there. I'll get back to you."

❖ ❖ ❖

A little later, Merton, Harris and Harlow were considering the news from Taylor.

"Morgan's okay in there for a bit. What do you reckon?" asked Merton.

"Well, I'm not sure now how much difference it makes, Sir," said Harris, "but his bank statements are quite interesting. They're in his name. Not joint. There's never much of a balance. Goes into the red quite a bit. It seems he gets three regular incomes a month. Pensions presumably. There's a regular monthly payment to a mortgage company and the usual gas, electric and phone. He draws out a regular fifty pounds in cash once a week but once a month that becomes a hundred and fifty pounds. I'd have to check back but I think they are all Wednesdays. Do you reckon that would bear out the blackmail theory, Sir?"

"It's getting less like a theory and more like a fact now, isn't it?" said Merton.

"Before we left him just now," chipped in DC

Harlow, "he said something about giving Sally the money."

"So he did," said Merton. "Let's not jump to conclusions just yet though. We'll take our Bruce Morgan a mug of tea. Peace offering. Well, it may be."

❖ ❖ ❖

The preliminary hearing of the charge against the gang of four jewellery thieves was the third on the list to be heard by the Magistrates. It all happened as DCs Oldroyd and Firth had hoped. They left the court building at about 1130 hours.

"Do you know what?" said DC Oldroyd, the senior of the two, "I'm not so sure that Merton's right, you know. He told us we needn't bother going back to the wood tonight. All the recent activity in Beech Street had put them off, he said. Well, there hasn't been any activity to speak of since Sunday when they took that ruddy mobile police station away, has there? Except for the raid on Tallows and that was at 1000 hours and specific to that property. I doubt our likely lads will be out of bed before midday. And remember what they told us that young lad had said? Something about seeing four of them going down the street and into the wood. It was before he had to go down for his tea or something. Before 2000 hours anyway. Last Thursday. I know it was bloody cold but the full moon and all that ... Nothing's certain but do you fancy giving it another go tonight?"

DC Firth considered the idea. "Yep, it's a long shot but why not? But, if you remember, on Tuesday night we went in a bit blind. We couldn't use torches, obviously, so we were blundering about a bit. I suggest we go and have a poke around this afternoon first, then get there around 1900 again. We'll get a better idea of how the land lies and find a better place to wait without having to hide in amongst those brambles for ages. I've still got the puncture marks."

"Good plan," said Oldroyd. "Let's grab a sandwich somewhere. Then we'll go and do it."

◆ ◆ ◆

DI Merton and DC Harlow returned to the interview room. Merton was carrying two steaming mugs of tea. He placed one on the table in front of his own chair. The other he offered to Bruce with the handle facing him. Bruce slowly brought both hands up to grasp the mug. It was a clumsy movement and he spilled some of the tea. He quickly put the mug on the table. "A bit hot," he said.

"Mr. Morgan, you will appreciate that, when we heard you say, on the recording of the 999 call you made, "I killed her, I killed her", we regarded that as a confession. What you are now saying is that you were feeling responsible for letting Sally Weston go by herself into that wood, the night before, but she did go in by herself. Is that right?"

The tone of DI Merton's voice was now less sharp and Bruce relaxed quite a lot. The slight slurring of his voice was now just detectable and he still spoke slowly. "I think that's what must have happened. I can hardly remember. I know I was in a bit of a state, seeing it was Sally lying there. It seemed to take me ages to get to the phone box. I tried to run. That was silly though, wasn't it? It wouldn't help her. All I could think of was that it was my fault, letting her do that. But she had done the same thing so many times and she had always said she was fine."

His voice began to break down again. "I don't know why I still cared … after all this time … but I did …. she needed … my fault anyway …"

"So, you say you had done the same thing many times?" said Merton. "Why was that?"

Bruce looked down. He sipped his tea, now his hand was shaking a bit less. "Well, sometimes when it happened we left the Thursday Club together and we said goodnight."

Merton leaned forward, "A short time ago, you said to me, "I gave her the money and then she went down the footpath". What money were you referring to, Mr. Morgan?"

Bruce Morgan looked as though the weight of the world had landed on his shoulders once more. He put his hands over his face to try to stop his emotion coming out.

DC Harlow stepped in. "It's okay, Bruce. Can I call you Bruce?" Bruce nodded. "It's just that we have to understand everything which went on surrounding Sally's death."

Now, Bruce appeared to want to unburden himself completely. He blurted out, "The money was nothing to do with her … her … being killed. I didn't kill her. Nothing. I used to give her some money because … because she needed it. She had problems. I couldn't afford it but she said she would tell my wife …"

"What had happened then, Bruce? What would she tell Jennifer?

The detectives decided to stay silent and allow Bruce to tell his story.

Bruce took in a deep stuttering breath, sighed and wiped moisture from his eyes with his right hand. His left arm was now hanging limp by his side. He was forcing himself to do his best to speak clearly and fully, at long last to explain to someone all about the burden he had been carrying alone for so many years. His speech was very slow.

"It was a long time ago. Sally hadn't long joined the Thursday Club. She was nice and we got on all right. I started walking her home, through the wood. There was a proper gateway at the end of the footpath then, until the council replaced the whole fence. I don't know why it was me. I know some of the others asked her. Of course, my wife ... Jennifer didn't know and it was innocent enough anyway. I just wanted Sally to get home safely. I know it was so stupid but one night it happened ... she ... she ... in the wood ... you know ... near where ... Anyway, Sally was pregnant and she had a baby. I never saw it. I have never been inside her house. She said she would never tell anybody who the father was ... but in return I had to pay to look after the baby. She couldn't afford to do that. If I didn't, she would tell Jennifer. I understood all of that and I didn't mind. I wanted to help. My responsibility. At first anyway. Then she said it was getting very difficult to afford to pay to look after her sister as well ... she said her sister was in a wheelchair. She needed more money. I didn't know what to do. They took the baby off her. Sounded terrible. She said she had documents to prove what had happened. Adoption or something. It was a nightmare. Went on for years. I kept it quiet ... Jennifer never knew. Then she wanted a hundred pounds a month. Too much but what could I do? I should have done something about it. But I didn't know what to do. I was a coward I suppose. It wasn't too bad till I was coming up for retirement. I asked if I could carry on working but they said not. Then, I really struggled. I could see the money problems coming. Pensions wouldn't be enough. So I lied to Jennifer so we could extend the mortgage on the house. The old car was falling to pieces and because I didn't need one any more to get to work we didn't replace it. No holidays ..."

He stopped speaking and then sort of wailed, putting his face in his hands again. "Ohh no, Jennifer will find out now, after all this time. She mustn't. Please, please ..."

"At the moment, Bruce," said DI Merton, I can't think of any reason why Jennifer should find out. In fact, I think she is going to be very pleased to have you back home. But before that, there's a few things I want to know. You said it was a hundred pounds a month. Did you give her a hundred pounds last Thursday before you left her?"

Bruce nodded.

"Where were you when you gave her the money?"

"We had an arrangement. We always did it on the first Thursday of the month. I got the housekeeping money out of the bank every Wednesday so on the day before those Thursdays I got an extra hundred pounds out. Jennifer never knew. I never wanted to give it her inside the pub. Didn't want to risk anybody seeing. So we usually left a few minutes apart and then we met up outside and walked part of the way down the footpath. Only part of the way now. Not as we used to in the beginning, you know, when I used to walk her home. Nobody else ever went that way. Then she carried on and I went back to walk home as usual. Years ago I always used to go through the wood with her but not the last few years ... I wish ... if I had done ... it wouldn't ... my fault ... I could have ... That's why I said I killed her ..." Bruce became emotional again.

"Tell me, Bruce, you gave her a hundred pounds last Thursday. That's a lot of money. What did Sally do with it?"

"Not sure ... oh yes ... she got her purse from her handbag and put it in that."

"Let's get you home," said DI Merton.

◆ ◆ ◆

DC Taylor now felt more relaxed, as she had offloaded the responsibility. She decided to defer any mention of support for Jennifer until she had heard back from DI Merton. The three of them were making small talk, a lot of it involving Joe who had made up his mind that he wasn't going to get a walk today, since his master had disappeared.

Taylor answered the phone when it rang. She smiled. "They're bringing Bruce home now."

❖ ❖ ❖

DCs Oldroyd and Firth had decided to grab their sandwich in the bar at the *George and Dragon.*

"Not a bad place is it, for a pub out in the sticks? said Firth.

"It's alright. This is the place where their murder investigation began isn't it? The Thursday Club meet here or something. There's a dart board anyway."

When Geoffrey, the landlord brought their sandwiches he knew, as landlords do, they were plain clothes police officers. He asked how the murder investigation was going.

"Oh, we're just passing through," Oldroyd said non-committedly. "It's not our job really but it's going okay, as far as we know."

Lunch done, they decided to walk from the car park of the *George and Dragon*, down the footpath to the wood, rather than drive around to

Beech Street. At all costs, they wanted to avoid any sense of police activity in Beech Street, especially today.

They squeezed through the gap in the fence. "This must be the place where the body was found," said DC Firth.

"Must be," Oldroyd said. He pointed to the right, towards the row of houses, the roofs of which could just be made out in the distance "For our job, we need to be over there, about half way between here and those houses. There's a big hollowed out tree, isn't there? Signs of activity around it. The lad, Pete, said he saw them come down Beech Street but I suppose they could have come from anywhere at other times. If we use this bit of a path we won't get tangled up in those sodding brambles."

Over to their left as they made their way along the little overgrown path, the diesel engine was clanking along with a train of wagons.

After a few minutes they came to the hollowed out tree. DC Oldroyd said, "I think we waited just over there on Tuesday night, didn't we? No wonder it wasn't very comfortable. Anyway, let's have a look around for a better spot. We need to mind where we put our feet".

"You never know," said DC Firth, "there could be some evidence lying around, linking activity to somebody, as yet unknown." He was having a look inside the hollow of the big, old and dying chestnut tree. He always carried a pocket torch and got it out to look inside the dark hollow.

"Rubbish, rubbish and more rubbish." Firth said. "How some people live. Hang on, what's this?" He leaned inside, reached down and picked something up, bringing it into the light. "It's a purse."

Oldroyd came over and they examined the purse, which was slightly damp and was made of a kind of patterned, coloured cloth material framed in a substantial gold coloured gilt metal with a clasp which was open. As experienced detectives, they instinctively only held such things by surfaces which could not hold fingerprints

"Anything inside?" The purse was empty apart from a single two pence coin stuck in one corner. "Weren't they saying something about a missing purse, back at the office?" Firth said. "Let's bag it and take it back anyway. Lost property if nothing else."

They continued searching around and decided upon a couple of more comfortable observation points for this evening. They would have to arrive in good time and wait hidden and in silence for a long while.

"Let's get back to the office and see if anyone

else is keen on joining us again."

"Maybe not after last time," grinned DC Oldroyd. "Anyway, I think they were going to nab somebody for that murder today, weren't they? They'll probably be busy with that. We'll see how they got on."

◆ ◆ ◆

A lot had happened that morning. By 1400 hours the team had got themselves some refreshments in their various ways and were now back in the office. The mood was solemn.

"Well, we were right about one thing," said DI Merton. "Blackmail. I think it's fair to say that Sally had been blackmailing Bruce Morgan and Jim Wheatland. Jim was a willing victim. His beer won't taste quite the same again. Bruce seems to have had some sympathy for Sally's plight but couldn't afford it. For ten years or more he had convinced himself it was all his fault and couldn't see a way out. She'd really got her teeth into him though. He's scared stiff of Jennifer finding out. For all we know Sally might have got her teeth into other Thursday Club members. Who knows who else? She used what money she needed to make sure her sister was okay and to run the house. She did it as economically as possible so she could stash the rest in that shoe box or the Post Office. We'll never know why she didn't put more of it in the bank. Who knows what she was planning for it? She certainly kept her plans to herself. We can be pretty sure that our Sally knew which side her bread was buttered on. The funny thing is, I'm not sure if I should feel sorry for her or not. Apart from the fact that she's dead, of course," he added hurriedly."

DC Taylor said, "She probably saw it as the only way she could manage. It sounds to me that it all started by accident, anyway, with Bruce ... in the woods. Then he wanted to do the right thing but got himself trapped. So it's been a very sad experience for him too. Sally just got bolder. And greedier. Yes, there may have been others but Jim Wheatland was the icing on the cake."

"Anyway," said Sergeant Harris, "We haven't got ourselves a blackmailer and we haven't got a murderer. Back to square one, isn't it, Sir?"

"Yes, to state the obvious, I suppose," replied Merton. "One thing I will do this afternoon is to go and see Margaret to explain where we're at. Before her brother and his wife go back to London tomorrow. DC Taylor, you can come with me. That money in the shoe box is now nothing whatever to do with any criminal investigation and never can be. It was just there in the house, wasn't it? So we'll take them an early Christmas present. Of course it's no replacement for Sally but it's bound to help."

"In a sense, Sir, couldn't it be argued that the money didn't belong to Sally?" DC Harlow said. "Jim Wheatland won't have missed it but Bruce Morgan's obviously struggling financially."

"Believe me, Harlow," Merton replied, "I've been wondering about that one since we first knew about that stash. It's pure chance we know about the money anyway. All we've done is keep it safe for a couple of days. It would be beyond me to know how to split it up fairly. I am no Robin Hood. I wouldn't even try. There could be all kinds of repercussions for us, for the Force. Trying to do it differently would be virtually impossible. Bruce Morgan and Jennifer will now have £100 more each month. That'll make a big difference and they'll survive. Margaret's sad life could be transformed. She clearly didn't know about it, sitting there in Sally's room. We'll keep it low key. Does that make sense?"

"Yes, I see, Sir. I think I get it. Thanks." said Harlow.

"Might as well go now, if you're ready DC Taylor? We'll retrieve the dosh from the property room on the way," Merton said.

Merton and Taylor were just getting ready to leave as DCs Firth and Oldroyd came into the office.

"You're all looking a bit glum," said DC Oldroyd. "something go wrong?"

There were brief explanations about the confession on the tape, the arrest and the revelations about Bruce Morgan's condition.

"Well," said DC Oldroyd. "We might have something to cheer you up a bit. The magistrates remanded our likely lads quite early this morning. That's one thing. Then we had a bit of a discussion. You know you said we shouldn't bother with the woods tonight, Sir?"

DI Merton nodded.

"Well, really sorry if we're out of turn, Sir, but we thought that wood might be worth one more go. I've had a bit of experience in the Drug Squad and you learn a bit about patterns of behaviour. Anyway, we decided to go and take a look in the light ... this afternoon ... because it wasn't easy to find decent observation posts in the dark on Tuesday night. So we've got a pretty good idea of the place now. By the way, if anybody wants to join us tonight, feel free." He was smiling.

Before anyone could say anything, DC Firth said, "We were poking about a bit amongst the rubbish and found this." He held up the evidence bag with the purse. "We thought somebody had said something about a missing purse. We found it in that hollowed out old tree, Sir. If it's just lost property we'll hand it in downstairs."

DC Taylor stepped forward and carefully looked at it. "It's Sally's." she said. "Definitely. Tapestry. Same pattern. Matches her handbag. Have you looked inside?"

"There's a two pence coin," Firth said.

DI Merton was thinking fast. "Well done. And I had always dismissed the idea that the murder was a random affair because Sally walked home through the woods. This could be drugs but it could also be murder." He slapped his forehead. "How far is that tree from where Sally was found?"

"I should think around two hundred yards to the tree," said Oldroyd. "As the crow flies. Further if you go by that little path. Then you'd have to sort of turn back on yourself where that bonfire's been. It's a bit secluded. Which is why the druggies use it."

"Right!" You always knew when DI Merton was calling the troops to attention. "Taylor and I are still going to see Margaret and take her the, er, parcel. If we don't get that done today, the brother and his wife could have gone back to London first thing tomorrow. They'll need to take charge of that money.

"While we're gone, Sergeant Harris, I'm putting you on the spot to organise tonight. Use the team. Organise an action plan. Get a map. Military precision. We don't want it to go wrong because we're only going to get one chance at this. Follow DC Oldroyd's advice. Position one plain clothes at various strategic positions to keep an eye and be able to nab them. Dark clothes. Put me with a good view of that tree. Uniform forming an outer ring. Everybody'll have to be careful how they approach and hide themselves. All cars well out of the way. We sort of expect them to come down Beech Street, like that lad said, but we don't know for sure. Any cars around that don't belong, even unmarked, would give the game away. Can't risk it. GP van somewhere half a mile away. We can call them in when we've nabbed them. Total radio silence till I give the order to move in. Might not need a radio for that. Everybody hidden in position by no later than, what do you reckon …?"

"1900 hours, Sir," said Oldroyd. "Oh, yes, make sure everyone knows to preserve any drug related evidence. Ideally before they see their chance to chuck it away."

"Okay, Harris? Any problems?"

"No problem, Sir," said DC Harris, hiding grave doubts but knowing that Oldroyd and the rest would be assisting him. The next few hours would be all systems go. "Only … er … hope they show up, Sir."

DI Merton added, "Too true. Oh, yes, mustn't forget, we want their outer clothes off them as soon as possible and into bags, labelled to the individual they're from. Use a description if they refuse names. Got to be watertight. Sally's blood could be on something. That might nail it. Don't care if it is cold. We'll give them something nice and cosy to wear in the cells."

"Taylor, do you have a car here?" said Merton.

"Yes, Sir, my Escort," Taylor replied, almost anticipating the question.

"We'll go in yours then, Taylor. We should be back within the hour."

◆ ◆ ◆

The inconspicuous dark green Ford Escort pulled up outside 66 Beech Street. DC Taylor rapped the door knocker. Graham opened the door and she and DI Merton, carrying a large carrier bag, went inside.

"We won't keep you many minutes," DI Merton said. "We just wanted to see how you all are. There's nothing specific to let you know about yet but we've been very busy putting lots of information together. I'm hoping to have some news soon."

"That's what you said last time," Graham said, in his usual rather off-hand manner.

Margaret was more grateful for the visit. "Thank you," she said. "It's okay, I understand. I'm alright, yes, really. Somebody's been around from the council talking about what help they might be able to sort out for me. There's going to be some temporary arrangement, I think, because Graham and Sarah have got to go home tomorrow. Mrs. Drummond, my neighbour, she's being really good too. But it's all a far cry from what Sally wanted."

DC Taylor asked what it was that Sally wanted.

The usually quiet Sarah, Graham's wife, spoke abruptly. She sounded somewhat angry, speaking harshly of her late sister-in-law. "She was a real pipe-dreamer. Sally. Lived on a different planet. She talked about Margaret and her living together in a little bungalow. No stairs she said. All mod cons, she said. In the country somewhere. Roses around the door I wouldn't wonder. All that sort of fanciful stuff. She had no idea how she was going to manage that, now did she?"

"Don't be too hard on her, please, Sarah," said Margaret. "She was trying to do her very best for me. She only wanted what was for the best. It was very hard for her. She didn't have much fun, did she?" Margaret's eyes filled with tears.

"Now, look, Margaret," said DI Merton, squeezing her hand. "Maybe the next time we come to see you we'll have some positive news. Oh, yes. You'll remember last time we were here, I took away a couple of items we found in Sally's room because we then thought they might have been involved in the crime. They've been examined and it seems we no longer need them. So we've brought them back. They're in this bag. Mr. Finlay, if you'd just sign this to say they've been returned. Fine, thank you."

Merton placed the carrier bag carefully on Margaret's lap. "Goodbye, just for now, Margaret. Have a safe journey home tomorrow, Mr. and Mrs. Finlay. We'll let ourselves out."

◆ ◆ ◆

DI Merton's left leg was feeling sore. Yet again he moved it away from the stray bramble stem he had overlooked when he had crouched down between two trees, almost an hour earlier. DS Harris had carefully given him a location with what would have been a good view of the hollow tree, had it been daylight. With his dark clothing, he felt adequately hidden, just a little way into the wood, to the left of the iron gate. It would be more a matter of sensing anyone entering the wood, rather than seeing them, although dim shapes could be picked out. A street lamp behind him threw a very faint glow, only just spilling into the wood. He could see nothing of the others.

He had revised his instruction to keep radio silence. Now it was to keep all radios switched off. There could not be the slightest risk of such a noise alerting anyone who might come into the wood that night. There must not be the slightest sound of any kind until he gave the word. He had a loud enough voice. There had been misgivings, of course. What were the chances, realistically, that the youngsters dressed in black, whoever they were, would actually come tonight? Although, thinking about it, he reassured himself they knew for certain they had been there last Thursday, not just because of the lad, Pete's story. Their presence then was now confirmed by the finding of the purse. Although, yet more misgivings, maybe it had not been them. Maybe it had been a random mugger after all who had robbed and murdered Sally. What of this master plan then? Where on earth would he take the investigation if there was a no show tonight? Superintendent Briggs would have quite a lot to say.

Once more, he looked carefully at his luminous watch. 1953 hours. He froze. To his right he sensed, rather than saw them come through the gate and walk quite confidently, weaving through the trees towards the big hollow one. Were there three of them? No, it was four. They were clearly talking to one another, though the voices were too far away to be able to hear what was being said. They were in no hurry, just ambling along, breaking off a twig here and there. Eventually, they were close to the big hollow tree. He only sensed where it was, within the darkest part of that area of the wood. He watched intently. No rush. Let them settle. Maybe they will sit down on one of those fallen branches.

A tiny pinprick of light showed in the darkness. A cigarette lighter, he guessed. Just another couple of minutes should do it, while they relaxed a bit more. Once again he convinced himself that they would not be a problem. After all, a few weedy, drug-riddled youngsters. Now was the time.

DI Merton stood up and at the top of his voice he bellowed, "Go!"

The wood instantly came alive. A dozen powerful torches lit up the area. A dozen police officers emerged from their hiding places and headed in the direction of the hollow tree, forming an ever decreasing circle.

As the young targets attempted to flee in different directions, there followed shouts of "Gotcha", "You're nicked" and, in one case, "It's your lucky day, mate. You'll get a night in a nice cosy cell." Another was told, "Terribly sorry, Sir. Have I bruised your wrists?"

Handcuffed and marched to the GP van which had been called in, they looked a sorry sight. In turn, uniformed officers removed each man's handcuffs, assisted them with stripping off their black outer clothes which were bagged and labelled with precise descriptions rather than names which were not so far forthcoming and in any case couldn't be relied upon. With handcuffs re-applied, each was bundled into the back of the GP van for their cold and uncomfortable six mile ride to face a night in the cells at West Divisional HQ.

Several police vehicles now occupied the end of Beech Street. DI Merton had been standing by the black iron gate watching his team. He would very shortly follow the GP van to Divisional HQ in order to process the evening's work and arrange to get the evidence analysed at the lab first thing tomorrow.

He was thinking through the day's events, asking himself if he could have done things differently. Not really, he convinced himself. Bruce Morgan had confessed, after all. There's no way they could have known he had had a stroke. Poor man, I've put him through quite a bit, to add to his other troubles.

As he watched, he noticed a light appear in the window of the house opposite, the one next to the big brown gates of Tallows scrap yard.

Someone looked out of the window and then the curtain fell back into place.

Back in the CID office, DI Merton said to the team, "For tonight and first thing tomorrow, I am sure DC Oldroyd will be able to lead on charging our four with suspected drugs or disorder offences. Only that, mind, at the moment. Strictly not the slightest mention of murder, or of Sally or the purse or anything to do with that. Those matters can wait while they enjoy their night in the cells. After we've assembled any evidence, we will see what tomorrow brings. Okay with you, DC Oldroyd, Firth?"

"That's fine with us, Sir. Strictly just the drugs." replied Oldroyd with his wide grin.

"Goodnight and really well done, everyone."

◆ ◆ ◆

At almost exactly the same time the four lads were being arrested in the woods, only a short distance away at the *George and Dragon*, the Thursday Club team were well on their way to winning their place in the next round of the County Darts League Championship.

Following a number of telephone discussions, there had been general agreement they should meet, in order to be able to properly reflect on the sad demise of their dear member, Sally. She would have wanted that, everyone said. Adrian was still in Spain. Bruce had earlier decided that he would go but, after the morning's ordeal, he really didn't feel up to it.

After the match, Geoffrey arranged for the entire clientele of the *George and Dragon*, in both the bar and the lounge, to stand for one minute in Sally's memory. After that, he organised a collection to support Sally's family. The proceeds of the collection were very generous indeed. Jim Wheatland made sure of that.

CHAPTER 17

In the office the following morning, Friday, DI Merton found that he still could not work himself up to get interested in whatever it was that a group of young likely lads got up to in a wood after dark, drugs or whatever it was. Maybe, he thought, such things were a passing fad, from having their origins in what had become known as the swinging sixties, free love and all that nonsense. Whatever they got up to was probably on a similar level, in his eyes, to the offences of causing an affray or riding a bicycle on the pavement. Give him some proper criminals, any day. All he knew, as he had said many times before, they just caused him a headache. They needed money to buy drugs and therefore more burglary, robbery, muggings, car crime and so on followed. It was that which kept him and his team busy.

In the ordinary way, he would usually leave the whole thing to a detective constable to cut their teeth on. As it happened, this week he had DC Oldroyd, with drugs enforcement experience, to deal with these guys in custody. How Oldroyd went about that was up to him and that was that.

In the ordinary way, Merton would keep well out of it. Except of course this wasn't ordinary. The whole point of last night's considerable operation was to try to flush out a murderer, no less.

DI Merton had wondered several times if Detective Superintendent Briggs had caught wind of the operation yet. The whole thing had been triggered by the discovery of Sally's purse in that hollow tree. Had he, DI Merton, read far too much into that? Had he automatically assumed too much? Was his decision too hurried? How could these lads know that Sally was worth robbing? Presumably she had died because she could identify them.

Ah, yes, the full moon!

Well, it was too late now for misgivings. DI Merton had done the only thing reasonably possible. He had withdrawn resources from much of the West Division for several hours. He hoped the Super's wrath would not be too great. What he needed now, after yesterday's slightly embarrassing blind alley, was a good result.

Now it was Friday morning again. Goodness, he was thinking, has a whole week gone by on this case?

As he was musing over these things, Sally's purse was being closely examined at the fingerprint bureau at HQ. If any of those lads' fingerprints were on the gilt metal frame of that purse it would certainly prove the robbery, for at least one of the gang of four. Surely it would therefore follow by implication that the robbers had murdered Sally. But he knew that such a fingerprint would hardly be enough for that. He tried to recall Dr. Franklyn's exact words when he had asked him if there would be blood on the assailant. What had Dr. Franklyn said …? 'Simple answer … I dunno … blood would probably have spurted but if he was holding that long-ish bit of wood, arm outstretched in a swinging motion. Jacket sleeves maybe. Maybe too far away, maybe not'.

DI Merton could only hope.

The area forensic laboratory was conveniently housed in the same building as the mortuary in Market Easterby. The evidence bags with the outer clothing from the four lads had been delivered there first thing that morning, personally by DC Harlow. Such laboratories were well used to every detective in the land wanting their results yesterday, as it were. The staff therefore rarely made promises. However, they could sometimes be persuaded to treat something as urgent if they knew that a murderer in custody being brought to justice depended on it. Harlow had been very persuasive and a promise of same day results had been made. Merton was thankful as he really didn't want to let these lads out of his sight until that matter had been resolved.

While pondering all of those thoughts, DI Merton had been alone in the CID office, rocking back on his chair. Indeed, he had been quite happy for the others to deal with those lads. He had instructed them to proceed solely on inquiries about drugs, breach of the peace and any such thing. No mention whatsoever of murder. Let them feel a bit more relaxed. In fact, there was no rush at all.

The door opened and the others came into the office. They all needed a brew.

"They're pretty hard work," said DC Oldroyd, grinning once more. "We let them have a nice leisurely breakfast. Hope they enjoyed it. Then, between us we interviewed them individually. They were saying absolutely nothing. Oh, yes. Guess what? One of them is our young friend from across the road - Mark Tallow. We nicked him the other day for receiving. He's out on bail. Well, he should be."

DC Taylor remembered that first time in Beech Street when she and DS Harris had knocked on the Tallows' door and the young man had answered it. That had obviously been Mark Tallow.

Oldroyd's grin got wider. "Tallow didn't like being nicked again. None of them like kicking their heels in here while we are pursuing inquiries. It's all very confusing for the poor dears. They don't know what's going on. Ha."

The phone rang. DS Harris answered it. He relayed out loud what the officer in the fingerprint bureau was telling him: "Several clear partial prints on the purse besides Sally Weston's, yes, from two persons, both on record, one person very recent, yes, Mark Tallow, 81 Beech Street, Millwood. Okay, and the other? Steven Handley, 127 Forest Road, Millwood. Thanks very much. You'll send everything through? Great. Cheers."

"Thank goodness these types never seem to wear gloves. They always seem to have their hands stuffed into their pockets, don't they? Anyway ... half way there." said DI Merton, sipping his coffee. "No doubt the lab will take a bit longer. Sometime this afternoon at a guess. I'm going to get an early lunch."

The others were discussing the case and things in general over their sandwich lunches. There was some tension in the air. This would be the day that this murder case would either be solved or move into a much more difficult and protracted phase.

"What do you reckon, Sarge?" DC Harlow said.

"Well, the fingerprints are a bit circumstantial, aren't they? They would probably say they'd found it lying around." Sergeant Harris replied. "Sally's blood on any of those garments would pretty much clinch it."

After a while, DI Merton returned, walking briskly into the office. He was approaching his desk when the phone rang. He grabbed it. He listened carefully for some time to what was being said, making notes. His smile grew wider.

"Got "em!" he whooped. "There's a lot of Sally's blood on one of the jackets as well as some on the trousers. Two of the others have varying lesser amounts. The fourth is clear but unless that one can prove he wasn't there at that time, as far as I am concerned they were all in it together. The one with the most blood will have been the one wielding the weapon. Guess who that is?"

"The bad boy seems to be that Mark Tallow," ventured DC Harlow.

"Absolutely right. He's the one with a lot of the blood stain and his prints are on the purse. Happily, the one with no blood traces is the other one with prints. That means we've got evidence on all four. As I say, they are all in it together but I'd like to have a cast iron case for the one who actually swung that lump of wood. That's got to be Tallow but we'll do our best to make sure."

DC Taylor, the least experienced of them all asked, "You'd have thought they'd have at least washed their clothes since last Thursday. They must have known there was the blood. What if they say they've cut themselves?"

"That's an easy one," Sergeant Harris said. "They're typical of the type. Spaced out junkies who wouldn't know a washing machine if they tripped over one. As for cutting themselves, all you've got to do is get them to show you where they've cut themselves. Then offer to give them the defence of giving a blood sample. Tell them that if their own blood exactly matches the blood on those clothes, they might be in the clear."

"Probably never gave a thought to whether they'd got blood on them, anyway," said Harlow.

DC Oldroyd interrupted and said he and DC Firth would be leaving them to it now. "We've got all we need to support the drugs charges, except they all clammed up when it came to revealing their suppliers. If you can get any of that it would be a real bonus. It's been an interesting experience. Hope you nail them. All the best. See you at the trial!" and they were gone, having completed their week's duty at West Division CID.

"Exactly," said DI Merton after they had left.

"Are we ready to go and invite them to confess now, like the good citizens they are?" His tongue was firmly in his cheek. He picked up a folder containing papers and photographs, putting it in his briefcase.

"We'll all be in on this but I'm going to see what Master Tallow has to say first, if anything, before we interview the others. It could happen quickly but I doubt it and so it could take a while, I suspect. DC Harlow, you saw the damage to Sally, at close quarters at the PM. You're with me, okay?"

"Count me in, Sir," said Harlow.

◆ ◆ ◆

Mark Tallow sat slumped on the same chair that Bruce Morgan had sat on yesterday. He had the appearance of a man who had seen the inside of this interview room enough times in the last few days and just wanted to get this over with so he could get out and return to his sad daily routine. Doing a few bits of acid and the rest in between collecting a few bits of scrap metal. He had decided that, like last time, he wasn't going to be here long. A constable stood by the door.

DI Merton and DC Harlow entered the room. They sat at the other side of the table and DI Merton put his briefcase on the table in front of him. Tallow raised one eyelid. The detectives introduced themselves and Merton expressed the hope that his cell was comfortable.

There was silence and no movement.

DI Merton said, "I understand you have been charged with certain drugs offences and that's why you are here, pending further enquiries. Is that correct?"

Tallow was clearly the silent type.

"Well," Merton said, speaking slowly and distinctly "I'm sure that matter is being dealt with and you will know very soon what the outcome will be. But DC Harlow and I are interested in a different matter altogether. On Thursday of last week a woman called Sally Weston was murdered in that wood, very close to where you were arrested last night. We are hoping that you will be able to help us with our inquiries into that. Would you like to have a solicitor present, Mr. Tallow?"

DI Merton allowed a few moments for a response. Tallow's body shifted slightly but he remained silent.

"You should take note of that, DC Harlow. We're taking Mr. Tallow's silence to mean he doesn't want a solicitor present, otherwise he would have asked for one. That probably makes sense to Mr. Tallow because he clearly wants to get out of here. Getting a solicitor in would mean some further delay because Friday is always a busy day for solicitors. They get all tied up on Fridays doing the legal stuff for a lot of lovely, decent people who are enjoying moving home with their lovely families. Decent, law-abiding people. Coming here would not be those solicitors' priority."

After a moment he went on, "Did you know Sally Weston, Mr. Tallow?"

He allowed a short time for a response. There was none.

"No? She was one of those lovely, decent people. She would have liked to move house. I'm sure you would like me to introduce you to her. Here she is."

Merton pulled the folder out of his briefcase, removed a photograph taken by the mortuary assistant at the post mortem. It was a close-up of Sally's face. He placed it on the table just in front of Tallow. There was barely a reaction. That surprised DC Harlow.

DI Merton was going to lay this on thick. "Well, Mr. Tallow, I can tell you that Sally knew you. In fact she knew you so well, she wanted to leave you a present when she died. When you swung that lump of wood at her face, wanting to kill her, and making that big, deep gash in the side of her head, her heart was pumping really hard for you. In fact her blood spurted so far out of the artery in her head, she left it for you as her parting gift - her blood is still all over your clothes. Wasn't that good of her, Mr. Tallow? Take another good look at Sally Weston. She's the nice lady who left you that present."

The detectives wondered if they could detect a slight movement in the man in front of them. He certainly wasn't going to say anything.

"And Sally was really generous with her presents because she gave a couple of your mates some too. Shall I tell you what I think happened? You can deny it if you want to of course. That's up to you. I think you and your mates knew that Sally came through the wood at certain times on certain days. Yes, I agree, that probably wasn't very wise of her but for whatever reason, that's what she did. She lives near you, just across the road. No, sorry, she used to live near you. She only had to live there because she had to look after her dear, disabled sister who can't leave her wheelchair. Obviously Sally can't look after her sister now. I believe that whenever you saw Sally Weston in the street, you noticed that she liked to dress in nice clothes and wore some nice looking jewellery. She carried a rather swish handbag which you thought might have some money in it.

"So, last Thursday you and your mates decided you wanted that money for yourselves to feed your filthy habits. You waited for her, surrounded her and grabbed her bag which she wasn't going to let go. You managed to open it anyway and got her purse out of it. Then, oh my goodness, your little brains suddenly realised there was a really bright full moon which lit up your little faces. Sally probably said something like, 'I know you. You're Mark Tallow. You live across the road'. In a flash you decided you couldn't have her identifying you. Oh, no. So, in a moment of blind anger, you grabbed a club - the piece of the fence which was lying nearby - here's a photo of it with Sally's blood on the end - and took an almighty swing at her head. You even had to do it twice because she defended herself with her arm the first time. You broke her arm by the way." Merton paused.

It appeared that Tallow had sunk even lower on the chair but he remained determinedly silent.

Merton continued, "Silly of you, wasn't it, to choose a night with such a bright moon? Anyway, what happened then? Sally Weston dropped to the ground. You couldn't see the deep vicious wound you had made when you had smashed her skull because her head was buried in a big patch of brambles. You didn't care whether she was alive or dead, although you really wanted her to be dead. So, like guilty school children, you ran away to that hollow tree where you like to hang out. You had a look inside her purse and you were amazed at your good fortune. Oh, yes, I know how much was in there. No doubt you split it up and then you scarpered. Am I about right so far? If I've got any details wrong, just let me know."

Merton stood up and stretched his legs by pacing around the room a few times while his words sank in. DC Harlow was, again, taking it all in and being impressed by his boss. But from Tallow there was nothing.

Still standing, now leaning over Tallow, DI Merton resumed his theme. "Okay, Mister Tallow. The way I see things is this. You have got to make up your mind and decide between three possible ways forward. It's entirely your choice. Aren't I generous? I don't mind which one you choose.

"The first you could consider is this: you say to me that you confess to robbing and murdering Sally Weston last Thursday, along with those three mates of yours who were standing by and letting you do it. You could include in your confession some details about the reasons you all had for doing it. While you're in confessing mode you could include full details about who supplies you with your drugs, couldn't you? And then you could sign a couple of statements. Job done. Easy. Then we could all go home. Oh dear, silly me, I meant that's just DC Harlow here and myself and this constable could all go home. Not you, of course. Do you fancy that option yet? Oh, yes, and we could tell the judge how co-operative you have been. It might mitigate your sentence."

After some more pacing around the room, Merton said, "No? Not that option? Okay, we could come back to it. But if you don't like that option, I'm guessing the second option is that you could try and chicken out and say you are completely innocent and that it was one of your mates that did it while it was you who stood by and watched. Before you get too excited about that though, you had better remember that there is far more of Sally's blood on your clothing than on any of the others. Two of them have just got just a few small splashes. They must have just been just standing around watching. Think carefully before deciding on that cowardly option because the judge and jury might not look at the evidence in quite the same way as you."

Another silence. Merton thought that Tallow would be keen to hear what the third choice would be. He was relishing the thought of telling him.

"You want the third option, then, Mister Tallow? Alright. Well, that might be an easy one for you. That's because it's quite simply to carry on with what you're doing right now and saying nothing. That's okay with us, you know. Makes life easier for us, in a way. We charge you with Sally Weston's murder. You'll spend quite a lot of time behind bars waiting for your day in court. We'll present the evidence to the judge and jury and we'll see what they decide. That's fair, isn't it? Oh, I nearly forgot. The evidence is not just Sally's blood you know. We've got her purse as well. A diligent constable found it where you thought nobody would find it. In that hollow tree. And guess what? It's got your fingerprints all over it."

There was a definite stirring from Tallow but, even after a couple minutes had gone by, he had still said nothing. DC Harlow was thinking he had come across many similar situations but, so far, they hadn't lasted so long and the stakes had not been so high.

"Alright, Tallow, I've helpfully laid out three choices for you. But before you make your final decision, I'll tell you something. You know what? I went to bed very late last night. Do you want to know what I was doing? Well, if you remember, you and your brother and your old Dad were in here the other day, charged with receiving. It was jewellery, silver and so on. Remember that? It's a fact. So you surely couldn't have forgotten that all three of you are on bail at the moment. Well, do you know what? All of that set me thinking there might be more to Tallows Metal

Dealers and the Second Chance shop than meets the eye. And then I remembered that my boss, that's the Detective Superintendent at Headquarters, wants us all to do our very best to clear up as many outstanding cases as possible. In fact he regards it as so very, very important that I had to attend a meeting about it at Headquarters no less, only last week. Some of those cases are quite nasty too. I'm sure you know the sort of thing? Robbery with violence, weapons being used, all that nasty stuff. They carry long sentences."

Tallow then actually looked up at Merton but still said nothing. A touch of panic could be detected in his eyes.

"So I spent yesterday evening going all through the files of outstanding cases, not just around here but in Central Division as well. It took me ages. Way past my bed time. I made a list, look." Merton took a list from the folder and waved it in front of Tallow. "Do you know what? I reckon a lot of those have got you and your brother and your Dad, yes, your Dad, written all over them. I guess it's just a matter of how much time we can spare now and what priority we give to chasing those up."

After another pause, Merton said, "Right then, DC Harlow and I will leave you for a bit of thinking time. It shouldn't take you too long to come to a decision. The constable here will keep you good company, I'm sure. We'll be back very soon. Come on Harlow."

DC Harlow opened the door and they were just on the point of leaving the room.

Tallow said, quietly but very audibly, "Not me Dad."

The detectives returned to their seats.

"No, me Dad had nothing to do with anything," Tallow said.

"I'm not going to be messed about at this stage," said Merton, displaying a touch of frustration. "As far as I am concerned, whatever we dig up by following up this list of mine, I think your Dad is most likely to turn out to be Mr. Big."

Tallow had changed. He was wringing his hands, his eyes darting all over the place. He was clearly wrestling with a big decision.

DI Merton encouraged him. "Well, it's not a difficult decision is it? You either did murder Sally Weston or you didn't. What's the problem?"

Tallow, in a few moments, had become a different character. Almost like a little boy ashamed of some minor naughtiness. "Okay, okay. I didn't know what I was doing. Yeah we wanted the money but that were all. I dunno know why I ... somehow ... she knew who I were ... didn't think ... just found the bit er wood in me hand ... can't remember doing ..."

"DC Harlow," said Merton. "I think Mr. Tallow has come to a decision. Take his statements. One for the main event and one giving full and complete details of his drug suppliers. Okay? I'll just sit here quietly, in case Mr. Tallow needs encouraging at any point."

"Yes, Sir," replied Harlow, reaching for the necessary stationery.

◆ ◆ ◆

Knowing they would soon be leading on the interviews with the other three, DS Harris and DC Taylor had been going over the details of the cases against them. Which direction the interviews would take would depend entirely on whether Tallow admitted to murder or, by implication if he didn't, then presumably all four would be equally charged.

"It's taking them some time, Sarge," said DC Taylor, which DS Harris thought was perhaps stating the obvious.

"He has his methods, Carol. Usually they're pretty effective. We can't count Bruce Morgan ... we could never have known about his stroke and all that but it does clear up the blackmail question. Hope his methods work this time. I can't really judge how Tallow's going to respond to a murder charge. Once Merton gives us the go ahead we can get to work. Those three are still in blissful ignorance, aren't they? Just in on drugs charges as far as they're concerned. I'm looking forward to giving them a big surprise."

❖ ❖ ❖

"Thank you, Mr. Tallow," said DI Merton, carefully stowing the completed statement forms inside his briefcase. "You'll be charged shortly. Take him down, constable."

As the constable was leading Tallow through the door, Tallow looked back and said, "You'll leave me old Dad out of it, like you said?"

DI Merton told him, "As I said, I'll review the cases on my patch - West Division - with the greatest of care and consideration. Of course, I can't vouch for my colleagues in Central Division where the most serious of those offences happened, I believe. That'll be up to them."

❖ ❖ ❖

During the following hour, each of the three lads were told that Tallow had admitted to murdering Sally Weston. They were told of the evidence implicating them. One after the other, each admitted their own involvement, signed their statements, were charged and returned to the cells.

Back in the office, the team had decided that whether or not there would be a specially convened Saturday sitting of the Magistrates' Court tomorrow or if there would be a wait until Monday, the four lads wouldn't hurt, getting used to life in a cell.

"After all that I think we deserve a cautious celebration," said DI Merton. "Anyone going to join me at the *George and Dragon*? They do a really good ploughman's."

EPILOGUE

Occasionally, the jet trainers still make a wrong turn and fly over the town and the diesel shunting engine still growls up and down the track with its clanking wagons.

Ultimately, Mark Tallow and his three mates appeared before the Judge and a Jury. They will all be spending a long time behind bars. In Mark Tallow's case, a very long time.

Bruce and Jennifer's life improved substantially as Bruce told her that it would now be possible to pay off their mortgage quite quickly. They would soon be able to afford an occasional holiday and a bottle of Bordeaux sometimes. Joe is much more settled, now that the routine of taking a daily walk with Bruce through the wood has resumed.

It would not be too long before DI John Merton decided to retire. Sergeant Dave Harris married and he and Susan live happily in the house they had selected. DC Richard Harlow still finds it difficult to find time for interruptions such as romance but continues to enjoy his football, his social life and being a conscientious police officer, which includes taking his sergeants' exams.

DC Carol Taylor's baptism of fire in the CID convinced her that she wanted to pursue her service in that role. She would go on to follow a distinguished career.

Old Mr. Tallow simply disappeared from the premises in Beech Street and the Second Chance shop in town closed down. The District Council cleared the scrap yard site, including the demolition of the two houses at the end of the street. Several modest homes, in keeping with the other properties in the street, will soon be built on the site.

PC Stevens now patrols the area a little more frequently and sometimes looks into the wood to see that all is well. Often, as he passes, he will acknowledge Mrs. Robertson as she so regularly cleans her front windows. While doing that she takes any opportunity to remind people of her role in alerting the police to the criminal activities in the wood.

With their sister's legacy and her brother Graham's support, Margaret now lives in a small, modern two-bedroom bungalow within a sheltered accommodation complex just off a leafy lane at the edge of town. All the facilities she needs are to hand. There are roses around her front door. She has made a lot of new friends there.

Millwood Town Council quickly installed three modern street lamps along the footpath by the side of the *George and Dragon*. After public consultation they tidied up the wood, repaired the fencing and designated the area a countryside park and wildlife reserve for local people to enjoy. Many local volunteers led by the members of the Thursday Club helped to bring this about and will play a big part in looking after it into the future.

The following August, at six o'clock one warm Thursday evening, prior to a reception at the nearby *George and Dragon*, almost a hundred local people gathered in the clearing in the wood, not far from the re-painted black railings in Beech Street. The Thursday Club members were all there. The Town Mayor made a speech and unveiled an impressive, substantial cast iron and wooden plaque which said, 'Sally's Wood'.

ABOUT THE AUTHOR

Douglas Maas

"From the beginning I only ever sought a quiet, peaceful, uneventful life but somehow a lot of extraordinary events just happened".

These are the opening words of Douglas's Autobiography - soon to be published (2022). It tells of his lifelong study at the University of Life. He has finally drawn upon this hotch potch of experiences and non-fiction writings to produce his first novel. He hopes those who venture into the tale will enjoy it.